HANDMAID

A play by
Jacinta Chaminade

Cover art by Aurelio Cruz Lorente
Cover Design by Francesca Funari

ISBN: 978-0-9983939-2-6

IMPORTANT BILLING REQUIREMENTS
All producers of *Handmaid* must give credit to the Author in all programs distributed in connection with performances of the Play and in all instances in which the title of the Play appears for the purpose of advertising, publicizing.

Represented by: aJENNda productions
https://www.ajennda.org
Contact jacintachaminade@gmail.com

"We live, while we see the sun.
Our life and dreams are as one."

Pedro Calderón la Barca

Table of Contents

PRODUCTION HISTORY

Handmaid received a workshop production at Florida State College at Jacksonville in April 29 - May 1 2010.

Handmaid by Jacinta Chaminade was first published in May of 2008 by University of New Orleans.

Produced by JACK - Jacksonville Artists' Company at Kent.

Book, Lyrics and music by	Jacinta Chaminade
Directed by	Roxanna Lewis
Rodriguez/Juan de Pareja	Nicolas Stephens
Diego Velázquez	David Hopcroft
Margaret/la Infanta	Ashley Reddit
Minerva/Maribarbóla	Sarah Bowley
Contstantine/King Philip IV	Steven Pedigo
Cachita/Reina Mariana	Harolyn Sharpe
Antonio	Devoy Johnson
Arvid Smith	Guitar, sitar
Kelly Sheffield	Costume Design

Handmaid - A full-length drama
Set in Little Havana, Miami

Cuban immigrant and fledgling artist, Rodriguez DeSilva has twenty-four hours remaining to fulfill the requirements of a commission he's received to create a replica of the famous Velázquez painting, *Las Meninas* in his dead father's honor. Rodriguez resents the project's requirement to paint a replica.

When pressure from his family and his ambitious girlfriend becomes too great, Rodriguez turns to drinking and painting everything but his commission, blurring the line between *Las Meninas*, his paintings, and the past and present. Visits from his disapproving deceased father and Velázquez himself don't help as Rodriguez struggles to find his identity, his artistic voice, and reality within dreams.

CAST OF CHARACTERS
(7 Actors)

RODRIGUEZ DE SILVA: A twenty-eight-year-old male. Cuban immigrant. Frustrated, undiscovered painter.
Rodriguez is also JUAN DE PAREJA, Velázquez's former slave turned assistant in the fantasy/dream sequences.

CACHITA DE SILVA: A fifty-four-year-old female, Cuban immigrant. She is Rodriguez's mother, attractive, blonde, heavy-set.
Cachita is REINA MARIANA of Spain from the painting *Las Meninas* in fantasy/dream sequences.

CONSTANTINE DE SILVA: A sixty-year-old male. He's a Cuban immigrant. Rodriguez's deceased father.
Constantine is KING PHILIP IV of Spain in the fantasy/dream sequences.

DIEGO VELÁZQUEZ: Sixty-three-year-old Spanish male. He is the seventeenth-Century Spanish painter of *Las Meninas*.
He appears in dream sequences wearing a mask when he represents someone other than Velázquez.

MARGARET CHILDS: Twenty-five-year-old, blonde female. She has childlike face and features. She's an aspiring playwright/musician and Rodriguez's girlfriend.

She is THE INFANTA MARGARITA, the central figure in the painting *Las Meninas*, in fantasy/dream sequences.

MINERVA TÓTH: Twenty-five-year-old, woman. She's 4'11" tall at best, unusually short. She's a dedicated and loyal friend to Margaret.
She is also THE DWARF, MARIBARBOLA from the painting *Las Meninas* in the fantasy sequences.

ANTONIO BUERO: Eighteen-year-old, male Cuban refugee, and Rodriguez's billiard student at the youth center. He's the reluctant guitarist for Margaret's play.

THE PLAY

ACT I

PROLOGUE:
MIAMI - 1997: RODRIGUEZ*

I: SCENE 1:
MADRID - 1663: VELÁZQUEZ & JUAN PAREJA*

I: SCENE 2:
MIAMI - 1997: MARGARET AND RODRIGUEZ

I: SCENE 3:
RODRIGUEZ & CONSTANTINE*

I: SCENE 4:
RODRIGUEZ AND CACHITA

I: SCENE 5:
CUBA - 1974: RODRIGUEZ'S CHILDHOOD*

I: SCENE 6:
RODRIGUEZ AND VELÁZQUEZ BILLIARD GAME

I: SCENE 7:
RODRIGUEZ & MARGARET - 1996*

◆◆◆ Intermission ◆◆◆

ACT II

*Indicates dream/fantasy sequence

A note about music for Handmaid

With the exception of *"Dame la Mano,"* which is a Cuban song in the public domain, all other songs are written by the playwright.

Handmaid is not a musical, the lyrics may be spoken, or sung a cappella.

If guitar accompaniment is desired, the character Antonio ideally would play the simple guitar underscoring.

Las Meninas - Diego Velázquez 1656
(Museo del Prado, Madrid)

For Aurelio Cruz Lorente, mi Rodriguez
-de tu Jacinta

PROLOGUE

RODRIGUEZ'S STUDIO:
LITTLE HAVANA/MIAMI, FLORIDA 1997

Rodriguez's paintings hang on
wall. Mirror on wall reflects
Las Meninas from his canvas.
Faint Spanish guitar plays.

MARGARET (V.O.)
We live while we see the sun,
our life and dreams become one
and living has taught me this

[Rodriguez holds palette
and brush. He turns around,
paints a large red cross of Santiago on Mirror behind him.
Light from behind Court
Door illuminates him.]

Man dreams a life that is his
until his living is done
and honey you taught me this
With your kiss
Qué toda la vida es un sueño,
y los sueños son sueños tambien

[There's a knock on the door.]

CACHITA (V.O.)
Rigo, the foundation directors have arrived. They've come to see your progress.

MARGARET (V.O.)
A little dust on the way, a frenzied extreme,
were We are year or a day?
Dreams themselves are a dream
Qué toda la vida es un sueño,
y los sueños son sueños tambien

[King & Queen reflected in Mirror. Velázquez in Court Door. Enter Margaret, in *Las Meninas* dress and Minerva in angel wings and *Las Meninas* dress. Rodriguez steps away from the canvas, holds up palette and brush. Everyone looks intently in the direction of the audience. Instruments sustain dreamy notes. Billiard balls clack. Lights out on everyone. Mirror is still lighted. All exit.]

END PROLOGUE

ACT I - SCENE 1

RODRIGUEZ'S DREAM
1656 - MADRID, SPAIN
PALACE OF KING PHILIP IV*

Red glow remains on the Cross of Santiago in the mirror. Velázquez's work hangs on the walls. Lights come up slowly. *Las Meninas* reflected in Mirror. The Cross of Santiago is absent from Velázquez's chest in the painting. The stage is dark. A light illuminates Velázquez's easel.

[Juan de Pareja stands in Court Door. Velázquez faces *Las Meninas* on his easel with his brushes and palette in hand. Juan crosses to Velázquez.]

JUAN DE PAREJA
Don Diego, it's magnificent!

VELÁZQUEZ
I'm quite pleased.

JUAN DE PAREJA
It is as if the Infanta is about to leap from the canvas to demand something.

VELÁZQUEZ
The Infanta Margarita isn't the only person in the painting, Juan.

> [Velázquez coughs, hands his
> palette and brushes to Juan.
> He wipes his hands with a
> towel hanging from the easel.]

JUAN DE PAREJA
She is the centerpiece of the painting. There is more light on her than any of the others, including yourself.

VELÁZQUEZ
Philip had commissioned a replica of a Titian. I was uninspired.

JUAN DE PAREJA
I've never known you to be uninspired.

> [Juan puts away brushes and
> palette.]

VELÁZQUEZ
On the contrary, I assure you that I'm quite inspired now. I found my painting.

JUAN DE PAREJA
That's not a replica.

[Juan points to *Las Meninas* on the easel.]

VELÁZQUEZ
I had to put the commission out of my mind in order to work.

JUAN DE PAREJA
The royal family is in dire straits. They can't pay the pastry chef! You don't want to risk displeasing the king do you?

VELÁZQUEZ
The replica is completed since long ago. In fact, it was while painting it that the inspiration came for this work, my manifesto.

JUAN DE PAREJA
Astounding!

VELÁZQUEZ
There now remains one ambition.

JUAN DE PAREJA
Your application for knighthood. The order of Santiago?

VELÁZQUEZ
Now I will focus solely on personal service to Philip. I've worked a lifetime toward that end, Juan. I will wear my Cross of Santiago. Parity, not painting, is my concern.

JUAN DE PAREJA
No bloodline nor royal order could endow a man with your mastery. Your paintings are important.

VELÁZQUEZ
Without the Cross of Santiago, I'm merely a court painter.

VELÁZQUEZ (CONT'D)
Acceptance into the aristocracy validates my nobility. I must
have it.

JUAN DE PAREJA
A man's worth is not rated by his family name. I learned that
from you.

[Juan rolls a cigarette and
lights it.]

VELÁZQUEZ
Why are you smoking Papeletes? They're for sailors and peas-
ants, not gentlemen.

JUAN DE PAREJA
I enjoy the tobacco, a luxury I have thanks to your generosity.

VELÁZQUEZ
One must smoke a pipe to enjoy the taste of the tobacco, Seville's finest product.

[Velázquez takes out his pipe
and lights a long stick match.]

JUAN DE PAREJA
You are Seville's finest product. Señor, the doctor ordered you
not to smoke at all.

[Juan extinguishes flame.
Velázquez, irritated, puts
pipe down on table. They
walk over to billiard table.
Velázquez pours two glasses of wine. He hands one to

Juan. Juan bows his head.]

VELÁZQUEZ

To the crown!

JUAN DE PAREJA

Indeed! To the crown!

[They raise their glasses up
in toast and drink. Velázquez
removes two cues from the
wall. He hands one to Juan.]

JUAN DE PAREJA

Has the king seen the new work?

[Juan nods to the easel on the
opposite side of the room.
Velázquez takes several shots,
then with the tip of his cue
pushes beads across a string
and marks his score.]

VELÁZQUEZ

No, not yet. After thirty-four years of service, King Philip
thinks of me as his confidant. As his painter, one would hope,
he trusts my sensibilities.

[He takes a third shot then
with his cue pushes beads
across a string to mark his
score.]

JUAN DE PAREJA

One would hope.

[Juan takes his shot.]

VELÁZQUEZ

I'm aware of displeasing the king only once. It was during our second visit to Italy. Philip only became disquieted when I didn't immediately return upon receipt of his request.

[Juan takes a second shot and marks his score.]

JUAN DE PAREJA

As I recall, Señora Velzquez also became "disquieted" when you didn't return!

[Velázquez laughs, takes his shot.]

VELÁZQUEZ

La Señora had no reason to be jealous. This old Spaniard had little to offer the Italian vixens we encountered I'm afraid!

[Velázquez's laugh turns to a cough.]

JUAN DE PAREJA

Don Diego!

[Juan rushes to him. He holds up his hand refusing Juan's help.]

VELÁZQUEZ

I'm fine Juan.

[Coughs again].

VELÁZQUEZ (CONT'D)

In Italy, the King allowed me to purchase what I wished for the palace. My portrait of you there is as fine as any of our purchases. Indeed, I'd like to return to Italy and buy it back!

JUAN DE PAREJA

I'm pleased that you find me a suitable subject. I've failed as an artist. I can't claim myself an artist by copying works.

VELÁZQUEZ

That is how I began. In the process of creating a replica, I recognized a shared humanity. Your humanity makes you a fine subject. That same humanity will make you a marvelous artist, Juan.

JUAN DE PAREJA

Those abilities are far from my reach. Like many things.

VELÁZQUEZ

On the canvas, I see myself as clearly as if I were standing in front of that mirror.

[Velázquez points to Mirror.]

On the canvas as on this table, I see possibilities and magical, inexplicable patterns. You see these three balls, a simple game.

JUAN DE PAREJA

The game is difficult. But the concept is simple: hit at least three cushions with your cue ball before it hits the third ball.

VELÁZQUEZ

Simple? The patterns are far from simple. They are, in fact, quite complex.

[Juan slides a ball in triangle
shape on the billiard table.]

JUAN DE PAREJA

How do you decide which path to follow? How do you determine the mathematical certainties?

VELÁZQUEZ

The art of the billiards is striking a balance between instinct and acknowledging those mathematical certainties.

JUAN DE PAREJA

Yes, if a level of mastery is reached. But not everyone can reach that level.

VELÁZQUEZ

The path of my cue ball can turn hope to reality and death to rebirth.

[Velázquez points to Hermetic wheel painting on the wall
behind him.]

Your people brought these ideas to Spain, yet you don't acknowledge their truths? There are limitless combinations on this wheel. These are the limitless varieties of life. The dream of lead being transmuted to gold, the soul being freed from an enslaved mind...

JUAN DE PAREJA

Slaves remain slaves even after they're freed. Some dreams remain only dreams. That's reality.

MARGARET (V.O.)

Qué toda la vida es un sueño y los sueños son sueños tambien

[Velázquez stops, listens.]

VELÁZQUEZ
Ah the sound of an angel's voice. Do you hear that?

JUAN DE PAREJA
Si, the Infanta enjoys her fantasy world. Her music occupies her often.

[Enter the Infanta and the dwarf, Maribárbola by the easel. The Infanta looks over at Juan and whispers to Maribárbola. Velázquez and Juan don't see them.]

VELÁZQUEZ
When nobody is looking at me, like now, I reflect on the question: Wouldn't music be the only possible answer?

[Maribárbola takes a gold chain with a satchel and quill pen from around her neck. Pulls out a tiny shred of paper and writes something on it.]

VELÁZQUEZ
How's your painting coming?

JUAN DE PAREJA
Painting?

[Juan chalks his cue.]

VELÁZQUEZ

Si, I saw you painting in the courtyard, captivated. Your subject was a mysterious, blonde beauty. The painting, in fact, was quite good. Who was the object of your inspiration?

JUAN DE PAREJA

It was only an exercise. I was trying to copy one of your paintings...

[Juan hesitates, shoots. King Philip and Reina Mariana are in the mirror. They stand behind the frame.]

KING PHILIP

Diego!

[Velázquez ignores the king. Juan whispers to Velázquez.]

JUAN DE PAREJA

Don Diego, aren't you going to answer?

[Velázquez reluctantly puts down his cue and walks to his easel. He looks in the direction of the audience as he addresses the King and Queen. They are in the frame of the mirror to simulate reflection.]

VELÁZQUEZ

Si, mi Señor.

KING PHILIP

I must have a word with you.

VELÁZQUEZ

Yes, of course.

> [They stand near the Infanta
> Margarita and Maribárbola.
> They look out into the audi-
> ence. The Infanta interrupts
> and talks to her father.]

INFANTA

Father, may I paint like Señor Velázquez?

KING PHILIP

Cielo, the world will never again see the birth of a painter like Diego Velázquez, I assure you. We are most fortunate.

INFANTA

But father, I want to paint all day, each day! How lovely that would be!

KING PHILIP

You may not, mi amor. Señor Velázquez cannot teach you to paint. He has other duties besides his painting to attend to as Royal Decorator of the Alcazar and Chief Chamberlain. We must prepare you for your future duties as Duchess of Austria.

INFANTA

Señor Velázquez! Father says I may not! Please talk to him! I must paint.

VELÁZQUEZ

One must listen to her father, your highness! He is wise and knows what is... best for his daughter.

MARIBÁRBOLA

I saw the portrait you were working on in the courtyard, Juan. It is of the Infanta, yes?

[Juan looks at the Infanta.]

It's magnificent.

JUAN DE PAREJA

It's nothing.

[Juan doesn't look at her.]

REINA MARIANA

[To Philip.]

Señor, what is the harm in allowing Margarita to paint? Have you seen her attempts? They are remarkably beautiful.

KING PHILIP

Nonsense Mariana! Have you lost your head? We have more urgent activities planned for this child. Must I remind you of her betrothal to her uncle Leopold? Just as you were betrothed to me, your uncle. One day she will not only be the princess of Spain, but also the Empress of Austria! The Hapsburg line relies on our daughter and her children. The Hapsburgs must endure.

REINA MARIANA
It is years from now that she's to marry. What harm would it do if it amuses her?

KING PHILIP
My priority is ensuring our enduring power. She is our only hope, Mariana. She has duties and familial responsibilities. Perhaps at a later time she can indulge dreams of painting.

REINA MARIANA
Don Diego, the king knows what is best. I hold your opinion in the highest regard.

[Velázquez, embarrassed, bows
his head to her.]

VELÁZQUEZ
I'm honored to be at your service your highness.

KING PHILIP
Have you offered an opinion about the talent of my little bufon that I'm unaware of Diego?

VELÁZQUEZ
Si Señor, pero, I know that the more important concern now is arrangement and decorations for the marriage of the Infanta Téresa.

KING PHILIP
Of course, you will begin planning the twenty-three staging posts for the Royal journey to the marriage of the Infanta Maria Téresa and King Louis XIV. A truce between Spain and France is only possible with the regal Spanish fulfilment of this magnificent union.

VELÁZQUEZ

I pledge my unwavering service. I pray that you will find the planned decorations acceptable.

KING PHILIP

Indeed. I see you've found some time to paint, Diego. You've produced only two paintings in eighteen months.

VELÁZQUEZ

Si, Philip. I've just completed a new work. I hope that you are pleased with it.

KING PHILIP

What is its subject?

VELÁZQUEZ

The worthy and regal, the disillusioned and unfulfilled.

KING PHILIP

What do you know about, the disillusioned and unfulfilled?

VELÁZQUEZ

Perhaps a little. They retain hope.

KING PHILIP

Nonsense Diego! You know nothing of them. You needn't concern yourself with them!

VELÁZQUEZ

Of course.

KING PHILIP

It is a remarkable painting however. You have shown only the back of your easel in the painting. Who are you painting in the piece, Diego?

VELÁZQUEZ

I'm painting you, mi Señor, of course! Who would make a finer subject?

KING PHILIP

A magnificent work. I shall hang it in my private chambers upon completion.

INFANTA

Pero, Padre, Señor Velázquez said I paint very well.

KING PHILIP

We'll not talk of that any longer, daughter. You have your court to amuse you, mi bufon!

INFANTA

Must I wait for everything I desire to fall from the sky?

KING PHILIP

Maribárbola, occupy yourself with my daughter. I'm putting her in your charge for the afternoon. Amuse her with a song or comedy.

MARIBÁRBOLA

Of course your highness! I assure you that her highness will be amused. The Infanta enjoys creating her own musical dramas.

KING PHILIP

Very well then.

INFANTA

Padre, please reconsider. I don't want to be a princess if I can't do as I wish.

KING PHILIP

Mi bufon, you are a princess. That is the reality. Someday painting will be a means for you to pass the time, pero, nada mas. Maribárbola, don't encourage my daughter's ridiculous dreams of being a painter.

MARIBÁRBOLA

Yes, your highness.

[Maribárbola bows and curtsies. She kneels next to the Infanta. Velázquez coughs.]

KING PHILIP

Diego, the Court Nobles have found more defects with your claim to parity in your application for the Royal Order of Santiago.

VELÁZQUEZ

I understood the process was complete.

[Velázquez's voice trembles.]

KING PHILIP

Another commission of inquiry has convened to investigate. I've requested papal intervention. I'm certain neither Jewish nor Moorish blood will be found in your ancestry.

[Velázquez coughs uncontrollably.]

VELÁZQUEZ

It is my dream, Mi Señor, to earn the honor of wearing the Cross of Santiago during my royal service as well as in my paintings, for posterity

KING PHILIP

I've done what I can. We shall see.

[Velázquez coughs again. Juan
rushes to his side.]

That sounds serious Diego. Have you seen the doctor?

VELÁZQUEZ

Yes, I have.

KING PHILIP

Perhaps you shall see him again?

VELÁZQUEZ

Indeed I shall, mi Señor

INFANTA

Buenos noches, Padre!

KING PHILIP

Hasta la mañana, hija mia!

INFANTA

Dulces sueños, Madre.

REINA MARIANA

Buenos noches, mi sueño bonito.

KING PHILIP

Come Mariana.

[King and queen exit. Reina
Mariana looks behind to
Velázquez. Juan pours a

glass of water for Velázquez. He takes it to him and puts a hand on his back. The mirror again reflects *Las Meninas* from the canvas. Maribárbola and the Infanta play quietly. Velázquez reaches into his pocket and pulls out his pipe.]

JUAN DE PAREJA

Don Diego, you should not.

[Velázquez lights it, still coughing slightly.]

VELÁZQUEZ

But I shall.

JUAN DE PAREJA

The inquiry into your bloodline will be completed soon and your name cleared of impurities.

VELÁZQUEZ

Perhaps the "purity" of my bloodline will only further ensure my life of servitude.

JUAN DE PAREJA

Soon you will wear the Cross of Santiago and paint it on your chest in this painting.

VELÁZQUEZ

How odd, Juan! Your Moorish heritage destined you to be my slave and yet, now liberated, you may paint whatever you wish, when you wish. You are truly free.

JUAN DE PAREJA

But there is much I will never be permitted to do. Think of the fortune bestowed upon you as royal painter. You paint important people that will always be remembered: popes, kings and infantas. You are one of them. Once the formality of parity is complete you will have proof. I couldn't dare to dream of that end.

VELÁZQUEZ

One day everyone in this palace will be gone, dust where our bodies once moved. Art will remain. I would rather be the first painter of common things than second in higher art.

> [Mari takes the little pad and quill out of a small satchel around her neck scribbles something on her pad and quickly puts it back in the satchel and down the front of her dress.]

JUAN DE PAREJA

You will one day be recognized as the first painter of all things, the greatest painter of all time!

MARIBÁRBOLA

[To Infanta.]

Come along your highness. I'll act in your musical comedies with the meninas.

INFANTA

But I must make Padre change his mind. I want to paint. Why can't we do what we want to do?

MARIBÁRBOLA
You will, I am certain. Señor Velázquez, Juan, hasta mañana.

[Juan nods absently. Velázquez
slowly bows. Maribárbola exits with the Infanta. Velázquez
coughs. He holds his pipe up
to the painting *Las Meninas*
on his canvas.]

VELÁZQUEZ
Thirty-four years of my life here Juan, painting their visions
of themselves, for them. How many do I have left? What do I
know about the disillusioned and unfulfilled? I may be one of
them. I await clearance for my Cross of Santiago, validation
of my very existence. Yet someday the bloodlines that dictat-
ed who we were will matter not. "Who" am I painting in the
painting, he asks. How easily he believed that it was he! How
fragile the regal ego! How easily he believed that it was he!

[Billiard balls crack.]

END OF SCENE

ACT I - SCENE 2

RODRIGUEZ AND
MARGARET - 1997

[Rodriguez, still in his apartment, is hunched over, sitting on a rung of ladder behind canvas holds palette and his head in his hands. He jumps up, disoriented. Mirror reflects a blank canvas from easel. He turns off the lights and exits his apartment. At the Billiard Center, Margaret and Minerva stand with scripts in hand. Antonio plays billiards.]

MARGARET

I told you, you can pull it off. Trust me. Come on let's go through it one more time. Then you can go back to your billiards for the rest of the day... OK?

[Antonio reluctantly puts down his cue and picks up his instrument.]

Try it again, but this time with a slight Bossa Nova feel. ...one

MARGARET (CONT'D)
...two and uhhh Dah dah duh dunt dunt dah dah, uhhh.

[He laughs and shakes his
head and starts playing the
song with a Bossa Nova feel.
He ends abruptly, tries again
and continues playing. Enter Rodriguez behind Mar-
garet.]

MARGARET
Scene.

MINERVA
It started right after mama died. Papa was drinking more and
more

[All notice Rodriguez except
Margaret. The guys continue
to play the same groove. Margaret looks on, nods her head
to the rhythm.]

MARGARET
That's it! I'm not playing with you! That's freakin hot!

[Antonio stops playing,
laughs uncomfortably. Rodriguez approaches Margaret
from behind.]

RODRIGUEZ
Baby! What are you doing here?

[Margaret turns around. Rodriguez kisses her.]

MARGARET

Hi.

RODRIGUEZ

[To Antonio.]

En qué andas?

ANTONIO

Bien, Tio.

[Apologetically, he shakes hands with Rodriguez.]

MINERVA

Hi, Rodriguez.

[Minerva looks down shyly. Rodriguez turns back to Margaret.]

RODRIGUEZ

What's going on baby? What's Minerva doing here?

[Minerva looks down at her script.]

MARGARET

Rehearsing.

RODRIGUEZ

For what?

[Then to Antonio.]

We'll start in a few minutes okay?

[Antonio nods, and reaches
for pack of cigarettes, puts
one in his mouth and crosses to Billiard Center door.]

MARGARET

The play! It won the contest! Remember? I thought it was
a long-shot when I entered. The prize is a staged reading
next month in the little theatre on Calle Ocho! Isn't that
incredible!

[She claps her hands smiling.]

RODRIGUEZ

Wow! I can't believe it! So soon?

[Margaret backs away from
Rodriguez, shrinks.]

MARGARET

Soon? Are you kidding, Rigo? I've been working on it for
over a year now!

RODRIGUEZ

I've been with you, the whole way, right? Still, it seems soon
to me. A year isn't that long. Do you think you're ready?

MARGARET

I'll make myself ready.

RODRIGUEZ

I read the draft again the other night. It wasn't finished.

MARGARET

Whatever! You aren't even excited about my news.

RODRIGUEZ

I don't get excited till I know things are certain.

MARGARET

Nothing ever happens if you wait for it to fall from the sky, baby. Would it kill you to show a little enthusiasm once in a while?

RODRIGUEZ

What does my guy have to do with all of this?

MARGARET

Your guy?

RODRIGUEZ

My student. Baby, come on. You know what I mean.

MARGARET

I asked him to work on the music for the reading. I need a guitarist, and he needs experience. Who knows maybe if it works out something permanent will come out of it?

RODRIGUEZ

I think that's a little premature. These guys just started a band.

RODRIGUEZ (CONT'D)
Besides, they already have challenges, like finishing high school. They need to concentrate on that.

MARGARET
You've been talking about how great he plays and how all he needs is an opportunity, someone to encourage him.

RODRIGUEZ
I don't want to him to have expectations and end up disappointed, or you, for that matter. This is too important for you.

MARGARET
How's the painting coming?

RODRIGUEZ
You're changing the subject.

[Rodriguez steps back to the billiard table, adds a note to the diamond-systems diagram on the dry erase board.]

MARGARET
I'm not changing the subject.

RODRIGUEZ
You are, as usual. It's not coming, at all. I don't even know how they can call it a commissioned work.

[He unzips his cue bag and removes his cue.]

MARGARET

It is a commission.

[He assembles his cue.]

RODRIGUEZ

Technically, yes

[She puts her hand on top of
his and stops him from con-
tinuing.]

MARGARET

They gave you the money up front.

RODRIGUEZ

Half of it, yeah.

[His head drops. She pulls her
hand away.]

MARGARET

Money that you already spent?

RODRIGUEZ

That's one problem.

[He doesn't look up. Minerva
eavesdrops.]

MARGARET

And the other problem is... ummm... that you still haven't
started the work, right?

RODRIGUEZ
Mag, is this conversation designed to motivate me? Because it's having the opposite effect.

[He takes out three balls, arranges them on the table and pretends to study them.]

MARGARET
Yes, it is designed to motivate you.

RODRIGUEZ
What are you trying to prove?

MARGARET
Minerva and I will come over and pose for you.

[Minerva drops her script. Margaret and Rodriguez both stop and look over at her. She dives to pick it up, flustered.]

MINERVA
I think I'll go and get some air.

[Exits and joins Antonio outside of Billiard Studio doorway with her water bottle.]

RODRIGUEZ
I don't see what that will do, baby.

MARGARET
Looking at living, breathing people will make you feel the ones frozen in the painting.

RODRIGUEZ
Christ, Margaret, the guy painted it over 300 years ago!

MARGARET
Then flip the foundation a big fat bird. Do your own painting. What are they going to do about it?

RODRIGUEZ
Are you freaking kidding me? Do you have any idea what my family will do to me if I screw this up?

MARGARET
Just DO something! What about your dream of being recognized as an artist?

RODRIGUEZ
I don't dream. I paint. This isn't a big opportunity.

MARGARET
I don't accept that! This is an opportunity and you sit apathetically by.

RODRIGUEZ
I'm not apathetic, Mag. But I'm not going to try to turn it into something it isn't.

MARGARET
Maybe someone will appreciate your work three hundred years after you die?

RODRIGUEZ
Mi niña, melodramatica.

MARGARET
You get a chance to have your work displayed publicly, to

MARGARET (CONT'D)

finally get the recognition you deserve but you say your hands are tied just because it isn't exactly what YOU think an opportunity should be. So make it one!

RODRIGUEZ

The foundation wants a replica of my father's favorite painting, to commemorate him. There will be a memorial park named in his honor, Constantine Alejandro de Silva Memorial Park...

MARGARET

He's dead.

RODRIGUEZ

...Then there's mama, who definitely isn't dead! Things aren't always as simple as, "follow your dreams."

MARGARET

But your painting will hang in the welcome center at the memorial park!

RODRIGUEZ

It's more like a tomb.

MARGARET

It's not a bad start.

> [Antonio and Minerva enter from outside through the doorway. Antonio gets his cue. Minerva gathers her things.]

RODRIGUEZ

You have to be intelligent. Plowing ahead my own way isn't.

MARGARET

So now I'm stupid for telling you to believe in yourself?

RODRIGUEZ

You're not being realistic, baby.

[Rodriguez reaches for her.
She ignores him.]

MARGARET

What does reality have to do with this? Anything's possible. Dreams transcend reality.

[Minerva tears a corner off of
her script, pulls a pen from a
long chain around her neck,
scribbles something on it,
and sticks it down the front
of her dress.]

RODRIGUEZ

You need to recognize it occasionally, mi cielo!

[Indignant, Margaret picks
up her gig bag and script.
Minerva looks down shak-
ing her head.]

I gotta work now. Antonio's waiting.

MARGARET

Let's go Min. (to Antonio) Thanks. We'll meet up here to-morrow OK?

ANTONIO

OK.

MINERVA

Bye Rodriguez.

RODRIGUEZ

Wait a minute. Here? Tomorrow? What's going on tomor-row?

MARGARET

Rehearsal. Your boss said he doesn't mind if we use the space when no one's here.

RODRIGUEZ

Scheduled rehearsals? Already?

MARGARET

No Rigo, I thought I'd sit around a few years and think about it first.

> [Rodriguez shakes his head.
> He kisses her several times,
> quickly and motions to An-
> tonio to come over. He chalks
> his cue.]

RODRIGUEZ

OK.

[He puts on a finger-less glove.
Minerva watches from the
doorway.]

RODRIGUEZ

Today I'm going to illustrate some mathematical formulas in the diamond systems of billiards.

MARGARET

[Rolls her eyes.]

The diamond systems.

RODRIGUEZ

The cue ball is going to hit the second ball and then travel to this cushion here

[He points with his cue.]

Then to this one, then here, before making contact with the third ball. If you follow your diamond system knowledge, it's a mathematical certainty.

[Margaret crosses to Rodriguez and stands between him and the table.]

MARGARET

No Rigo! You're explaining it all wrong. Here guys, let me illustrate for you.

[She takes two balls off the

table and holds them up to
Antonio.]

MARGARET

Think of it this way: Imagine this ball here is a guy, and this
ball here is his girlfriend,

[She turns to diamond systems poster.]

and these three cushions are huge, no... colossal, opportunities. Now, if he grazes his girlfriend, like this,

[She slides one of the balls
along the lines on the poster.]

and bounces off this opportunity, then the next, steadily los-
ing speed and force...

[She turns back to Antonio.]

MARGARET

...it's a mathematical certainty that they will break up and
nothing good will happen to him ever again!

[Margaret slams two balls
down on the table, picks up
her things and exits. Minerva
leaves behind her, shrugging
her shoulders.]

RODRIGUEZ

[To himself.]

RODRIGUEZ (CONT'D)
Ay ya yaay! Sorry about that Antonio. Margaret gets a little dramatic sometimes.

> [He makes a few shots ag-
> gressively, then stops and
> disassembles his cue.]

We'll get an early start next week. I think you've had ah... enough on your plates for one day anyway. OK?

ANTONIO
Yeah, it's cool.

RODRIGUEZ
Besides you have your S.A.T. test soon don't you?

ANTONIO
No joke. Unfortunately.

RODRIGUEZ
You'll be fine. I can help with math or English, whatever you need. Don't hesitate to ask OK?

ANTONIO
Yeah, of course man. We're cool.

RODRIGUEZ
Don't overdo it this weekend. You gotta do well on the test.

ANTONIO
All right man.

RODRIGUEZ
I'm serious. It's important.

RODRIGUEZ

Yeah, OK.

> [Antonio exits. Rodriguez pulls a pack of tobacco out of his pocket, rolls cigarette. As he licks the cigarette paper he studies table, puts balls under the table and drapes a cover over it. He examines the diamond systems poster, turns out the lights, exits and locks the door.]

END OF SCENE

ACT I - SCENE 3

RODRIGUEZ AND CONSTANTINE*

Rodriguez's Apartment-Sound of keys opening door.

[Rodriguez enters apartment from darkness. He stops, stares at easel.]

Empty liquor bottles, Chinese take-out containers, pizza boxes and piles of clothes everywhere. Constantine and Cachita stand behind the frame of the mirror they are a reflection of Rodriguez's canvas.

[He crosses directly to the canvas and paints more of the portrait of Constantine. Two artist's mannequins propped the easel. A foam-board-backed poster of *Las Meninas* leans against wall on the floor

beside him. A painting of
Margaret hangs on the wall.

MARGARET (V.O.)
A king dreams he's king and he lives, in the deceit of a king,
commanding and governing.
And all the praise he receives written in wind and leaves,
and honey I taught you this with my kiss:
Qué toda la vida es un sueño y los sueños son sueños tambien.

[From behind the frame of
the mirror Constantine reads
the newspaper. Cachita is beside him, expressionless.]

MARGARET (V.O./SUNG)
Qué toda la vida es un sueño y los sueños son sueños tambien

CONSTANTINE
So, Rodriguez, big article here about this project. You're getting pretty good at chasing dreams to avoid real work, eh?

[Rodriguez faces the easel.]

RODRIGUEZ
I don't dream, Papa. It's just an article about your memorial
park and your beloved painting, "*Las Meninas.*"

[He flips his hand toward the
poster of *Las Meninas.*]

CONSTANTINE
The most beautiful painting by the world's greatest artist, my
favorite painter.

[Constantine points to the
poster of *Las Meninas* from
behind his frame.]

It's inconceivable that any novice today could create something of that magnitude.

RODRIGUEZ

This "novice" hasn't painted a stroke for the commission
yet. So you may be worried about my painting disappoint-
ing you for nothing!

CONSTANTINE

Velázquez was brilliant. He was financed Rodriguez, royal painter to the king! Money is power. You have to work
hard and help others fulfil their dreams. That is what I did
so we could come here. But, look at this article! To read
this interview you'd think YOU paddled yourself here
from Cuba!

[Rodriguez takes a swig. He
shrinks.]

Does that look like the face of an artist who's hungry, living
in a run down apartment? No! You need to work. Worry
about art later.

RODRIGUEZ

I do work!

CONSTANTINE

Chita, do you hear your son? He calls shooting pool with
street rats a few times a week work!

RODRIGUEZ
Billiards, Papa.

CACHITA
He is putting a lot of effort into the boys, Papa. He's working very hard.

RODRIGUEZ
I support their ideas, teach them the discipline of the sport and its mathematical principles. I listen to them.

CONSTANTINE
You're no further along than they are!

CACHITA
Your father only wants what's best, Rigo. He worked your whole life to give you more opportunities for success than those boys had.

RODRIGUEZ
I didn't want to leave, mama! At least back home they had an education. Art wasn't a luxury for the rich.

CONSTANTINE
Back home? Home? This is home! My education in Cuba didn't get us a new Cadillac. Or a big house with air conditioning, did it? You seemed to enjoy those amenities when we came here, amenities provided to you through my hard work!

RODRIGUEZ
I'm trying to do what YOU want.

CONSTANTINE
Working with menaces to society? It's practically volunteer

CONSTANTINE (CONT'D)
work. Your salary is nothing! You're not even financially sta-
ble.

RODRIGUEZ
I understand them.

CONSTANTINE
I won't allow you to undermine years of building the family name with your ridiculous, selfish notions of becoming a
painter!

RODRIGUEZ
I'm not "becoming a painter," Papa, I am painter!

CONSTANTINE
Don't embarrass me with this foundation commission. Just
do a simple replica. It's only a painting of a painting.

CACHITA
Papa, be reasonable. He has considerable talent. It's who he is.

CONSTANTINE
Chita have you lost your head? He has no idea who he is!

[Cachita fights back tears.]

RODRIGUEZ
I used to give my paints to mama to keep hidden in a box so
you wouldn't find them. Did you know that?

CONSTANTINE
Listen to me very carefully, there will never be another
Velázquez.

[Constantine and Cachita
freeze. Rodriguez finishes the
portrait of his father. He removes it from the easel and
hangs it on the wall. He sits
down on ladder rung and
stares at the easel. Lights fade
on his parents. Nothing is reflected now in the Mirror. He
swills his rum.]

RODRIGUEZ

Mag's right. I should flip em a "big bird" and paint my own
interpretation. ...Mag. Mag!

[He lights his cigarette and
walks over to the *Las Meninas* poster. He's unsteady. He
points to Velázquez in the
painting.]

Royalty? Kings? Fucking royal courts and princesses? Look at
this guy! He's got it made.

[He smokes, pours himself a
shot of Rum, staggers over to
one of the mannequins.]

A dance señorita?

[He sings, picks up a mannequin and slow dances.]

RODRIGUEZ (SUNG)

Dame la mano, daaaaaaaaahme la mano... la da da da da... mi

RODRIGUEZ (CONT'D)
corozon! (spoken) Whaat did you say Señorita? You think I'm a great dancer? Hmmm. Margaret used to say that. She's not saying that now. Nope. Not anymore. Nunca.

[He looks at the painting of Margaret on the wall.]

Oh, you think I'm cute tambien? De verdad?

[He puts the mannequin down, laughs.]

Sorry baby... no depth!

[He returns to his easel. He picks up his paintbrush and stares at the blank canvas. He puts the brush down. He walks next to the poster of *Las Meninas.*]

And what do you say, Señor Velázquez, of what my father calls my "ridiculous dreams of being a painter"?

RODRIGUEZ (AS VELÁZQUEZ)
Why your talent is magnificent Rodriguez, and your dream, in fact, quite attainable.

[Rodriguez laughs hysterically. He's drunker. He stops laughing and turns around to the painting of his father on the wall. He turns back to *Las Meninas* and laughs more.]

RODRIGUEZ (CONT'D)

I knight you Rodriguez de Silva. On behalf of myself and with the blessing of King Philip, to whom I am but a humble servant, the Cross of Santiago!

> [Rodriguez dips his brush into red paint and paints a cross on his own chest.]

I, Diego Velázquez do hereby recognize the magnificence, sophistication and insight of your work. And you didn't even have to kiss any royal ass! Remarkable.

> [Rodriguez laughs, pours a drink and rolls a cigarette. He holds up his glass, almost spilling its contents, in a mock toast.]

Here's to you Papa, King Constantine! If they turn me down tomorrow, I'll piss in your park!

> [Rodriguez staggers over to the *Las Meninas* poster and kicks it over. He kicks the mannequins onto the floor. He throws his paints and brush violently. He laughs and falls on the floor with the mannequins.]

Did you hear me Papa? I'll piss in your fucking park!

END OF SCENE

ACT I - SCENE 4

CACHITA AND RODRIGUEZ

[Rodriguez lies in the pile of paints, the poster, canvases and mannequins, and bottles on the floor. There is a knock on the door. He pops his head up, startled.]

RODRIGUEZ

Qué?

[He gets up in obvious pain and pours rum into a glass. He walks to the mirror and looks at himself. He walks to the door.]

Okay, okay, I'm coming!

[He looks through the peep hole. His head drops. He moves away from the door and shoves some of the mess in piles. There is another knock on the door.]

RODRIGUEZ (CONT'D)

[To himself]

Shit!

[He pulls a garbage can over to a table and in one fluid movement of his arm, pushes bottles and ashtrays and mess into the can. Cachita calls to him from outside the door.]

CACHITA

Rigo?

[There is a third knock on the door. Rodriguez covers the blank canvas and easel with a sheet, goes to the door, opens it. Cachita is there with a pot in her arms.]

RODRIGUEZ

Mama!

[He takes the pot from her and kisses her on each cheek. He hesitates to back up and let her in. She looks over his shoulder into his apartment and he retreats.]

RODRIGUEZ

Como estas?

[She walks past him into the
apartment. She pulls out a fan
and snaps it open.]

CACHITA

I hate this heat. It's going to kill me!

[She walks past him flipping
her fan dramatically.]

RODRIGUEZ

What's all this?

CACHITA

Ropa vieja y frijoles negros.

[She unties the scarf from
under her chin, takes it off
her head and starts to put it
down on the table, picks up a
Chinese food container, and
drops it in the garbage can.
Rodriguez looks around at
the mess.]

RODRIGUEZ

Mama, please!

[Cachita puts her scarf over
the back of a chair.]

CACHITA
I thought you could use a home-cooked meal.

RODRIGUEZ
Thanks, Mama. It wasn't necessary.

CACHITA
I've been calling for days Rigo. When you didn't answer I got worried and decided to come over.

[She continues clearing the trash off the table.]

RODRIGUEZ
Really?

CACHITA
You didn't get any of my messages?

RODRIGUEZ
Huh? Weird.

[He takes out his paints and supplies. He busies himself arranging them and flips through a sketch pad.]

Well, I'm fine. Just busy working...

CACHITA
Si, claro.

[Cachita puts her fan down on the chair. She takes an

apron out of her bag and ties
it around her waist.]

How's the commission painting coming, mi hijo?

RODRIGUEZ

Great. Fine.

[Cachita cleans the table and
puts a cloth over it. She takes
out a covered plate, and sil-
verware from her bag and
sets them on the table. Rodriguez walks over to her. She
takes his face in her hands.]

RODRIGUEZ

Mama, please... you don't have to...

CACHITA

Mira! You look like you haven't eaten or slept in weeks! Sit
down and eat.

[She pushes him insistently
into a chair.]

RODRIGUEZ

I'll eat later Mama, I'm not hungry. You shouldn't have gone
to all this trouble.

CACHITA

Trouble, to cook for my son from time to time?

[She uncovers the plate of

> food looks at the poster of
> *Las Meninas* and the man-
> nequins on the floor, then, at
> Rodriguez's easel.]

Besides, they completed the final touches for the opening of the park last week so the foundation wants to come over to-morrow to check on your progress with the painting and I thought I should...

RODRIGUEZ
Tomorrow? What? No I can't. I... I won't even be here.

CACHITA
I'll use my key and show them the painting. We should clean up this place first, after you eat. Eat Rigo!

RODRIGUEZ
Mama, please.

CACHITA
They are excited to see your progress. Imagine a park named in your father's memory, his son's painting on permanent dis-play. That's quite an honor, no?

RODRIGUEZ
Si, for papa. Constantine Alejandro DeSilva Park! Even dead he's recognized for his achievements!

> [Rodriguez flips his hand at
> his father's framed portrait on
> the wall. Cachita also pauses
> and looks at it expressionless.]

RODRIGUEZ

I could be anybody, Mama. It doesn't matter who paints the replica. It doesn't really matter who I am.

CACHITA

Look mi hijo you aren't just anybody. You are the son of Constantine DeSilva!

RODRIGUEZ

You said it yourself. I'm "the son of Constantine DeSilva." That's who I am.

[He begins eating. Cachita
looks away, says nothing.]

CACHITA

[Forcefully she spoons more
onto his plate.]

Do you plan to get discovered by barricading yourself in here never showing your work to anyone?

RODRIGUEZ

I don't plan. I paint. I don't think about being discovered. It's not up to me.

CACHITA

How's work? Are the niños doing better?

RODRIGUEZ

They're not exactly niños mama. Teenage boys, no one cares about.

CACHITA

They have families, don't they?

RODRIGUEZ

Antonio floated here on a tire. Half of his family is still in Cuba.

> [Cachita gets an ironing
> board out and irons madly.]

Javi, came here on his own after his father abandoned him. He's never even known his father! I can't imagine how that feels.

> [Cachita wipes the sweat
> from her forehead with her
> apron.]

His mama came after. She works three jobs just to take care of him and his sisters. She doesn't even speak English. She doesn't have time... Mama?

> [He looks at Cachita. She is
> lost in thought. She burns her
> finger and drops the iron on
> the floor.]

CACHITA

Ay!

> [She shakes out her left hand
> and sticks her ring finger in
> her mouth.]

RODRIGUEZ

Mama!

[He runs to her. He picks the
iron off the floor.]

CACHITA

I'm fine. Mi hijo. It's nothing. Go! Eat!

[Rodriguez stares at her, per-
plexed and reluctantly returns
to his seat. She resumes ironing. She looks at the painting
of Margaret on the wall.]

CACHITA

Where's Margaret been?

RODRIGUEZ

She's busy. That's all.

[She stops ironing and looks
at him.]

CACHITA

Mira, Rigo, I know you're talented. But patrons don't listen to
the mamas of artists. If they did, you'd be the most patronized
artist in all of Little Havana!

[She returns to ironing.]

RODRIGUEZ

The foundation doesn't consider me an artist. I don't choose
what to paint - or anything - for that matter.

[Rodriguez shrinks down
into his seat. Cachita stands
behind him. She looks up at

the portrait of Constantine,
then down at her son loving-
ly.]

CACHITA

This is a chance to show what you can do. Who knows what
doors may open? Look at your portrait of your father, Rigo!
It's the work of a great artist.

RODRIGUEZ

Mama, everything's fine, really. It can't be tomorrow. That's
all I said.

CACHITA

The foundation has a right to come if they want to. I can't
stop them. You're twenty-nine, son. Do you know what that
means?

[Rodriguez shrinks into his
seat.]

That means you have less than an hour for each year of your
life till the board members come here to see your progress!

[Cachita smiles and winks.]

RODRIGUEZ

Thanks mama, it sounds even more impossible when you put
it that way! The foundation operates like papa. King Constantine wins again.

CACHITA

Your father wasn't a monster. He worked hard to earn what
we have now.

[Cachita hangs the pants and shirt on a hanger. She begins to clear the table.]

RODRIGUEZ

Mama, I'll do it.

[Rodriguez stops eating and stands up, takes her head scarf off the chair to hand to her. Cachita ignores the gesture and continues cleaning.]

CACHITA

It won't take long!

RODRIGUEZ

I'm gonna work now. I'll do it myself later, please.

[She reluctantly unties her apron and puts it in her bag. He helps her collect her things.]

CACHITA

OK, pero soy tu madre. Escuchame!

[Cachita flips her fan open again.]

RODRIGUEZ

Si, si, claro. Besitos Mama.

[Rodriguez kisses Cachita.]

CACHITA

Don't forget to eat your tres leches, it's your favorite.

RODRIGUEZ

I'll eat it don't worry, vale vale!

CACHITA

I'll see you tomorrow night then with the foundation. Be here. Rigo, have something ready for them to see.

> [Rodriguez opens the door
> for her.]

RODRIGUEZ

I'm trying not to let anybody down.

> [Cachita's tone is reproach-
> ful.]

CACHITA

You better do more than try! You are representing the family. This is important.

> [Cachita looks over at the ea-
> sel and begins dramatically
> fanning herself again.]

CACHITA

Hasta mañana! Este calor me va a matar!

RODRIGUEZ

Bye Mama, besitos!

> [Cachita reluctantly exits.]

CACHITA (V.O.)

Besitos mi Rigo!

> [Rodriguez shuts the door
> and falls back against it. He
> picks up his drink and takes
> a swig. He walks over to the
> easel and removes the sheet.
> A blank canvas is reflected in
> the mirror. He turns to the
> wall and talks to the portrait
> of his father.]

RODRIGUEZ

I bet you're laughing like hell watching us jump through hoops for you, huh papa? Would it have been so hard for you to smile at her once in a while? Would it have killed you to tell her she looked pretty from time to time? Even dead your blood boils. Did you hate me so much that you had to take it out on her?

END OF SCENE

ACT I - SCENE 5

HAVANA, CUBA 1974:
RODRIGUEZ'S CHILDHOOD*

Billiard balls crack.

[Rodriguez sits on the ladder
and stares at blank canvas. He
takes another sip of his drink.
Antonio plays guitar (song:
"Dame la Mano").]

ANTONIO (SUNG)
Quisiera Qué mis cantares
Nacidos del corazon
Lo guarde como un ofrenda de mi amor hacia ti
Para Qué nunca te olvides
Dame la mano, amigo mio del corazon
Tu eres la luz Qué me alumbra
Dame La Mano

[Cachita enters. She wears
an apron and is younger. She
puts a table cloth over the billiard table. Rodriguez slowly
walks over to her and helps
her set the table.]

Y caminemos por el sendero qué conce a la felicidad
Qué los dias qué no quéden sean felices para ti
Caminemos caminemos mucho mas
Dame la mano, qué me vengo cayendo.

> [Velázquez enters. He wears
> a masquerade mask. He car-
> ries a small child-sized easel
> and a bouquet of flowers. He
> gives the flowers to Cachita.
> She puts them in a vase and
> places the vase on the ta-
> ble. She looks down, embar-
> rassed, when he tries to kiss
> her and nods to Rodriguez.]

Quisiera qué mis cantares
Nacidos del corazon
Lo guarde como un ofrenda de mi amor hacia ti
Para qué nunca te olvides

> [Velázquez sets up the ea-
> sel, and hands Rodriguez a
> palette and paint brush. He
> instructs him as Rodriguez
> paints. Rodriguez turns to
> him mesmerized.]

CACHITA

I knew he was the one, the love of my life. But what could
I do? He had nothing except his paintings and dreams. He
loved me though, I knew that.

> [Rodriguez paints on a pa-

per on the little easel. Cachita gently puts her hand on
Velázquez' shoulder and motions to the door for him to
leave. She kisses Rodriguez
and sends him off too. He
slowly walks to the large easel in his studio Turns back to
watch his mother.]

CACHITA (CONT'D)
Then I met Constantine Alejandro de Silva, full of ambition
and confidence. He said could take us to the land of opportunity. He asked me to be his wife. So I let go of the man of my
dreams. And I waited. I cooked, I cleaned, and I waited for you.

[Enter Constantine. He is
younger with his hair slicked
back. Slowly Cachita pours
wine in a glass on the table.
She serves Constantine.]

ANTONIO (SUNG)
*Dame la mano, amigo mio del corazon Tu eres la luz qué me
alumbra Dame La Mano*

[Music continues. Volume
increases. Constantine points
to the little easel, pulls off a
painting, holds it up to Cachita and shakes it.]

CONSTANTINE
What the hell is this Chita?

[He crumples up Rodriguez'
artwork. She takes it from him
and straightens it out carefully
on the table.]

He was here, wasn't he!

[She pleads with him to be
quiet and motions for him
to sit back down at the table.
He points to the vase of flowers. He stands up, hits it, and
sends it flying off the table.]

This is how you repay me for my hard work? He comes to my
home when I turn my back? Soon we'll be far away from him?
We will never see him again.

[He grabs her shoulders and
pushes her against a wall, he
takes the back of his hand
and slaps her across the face.]

Do you understand me Chita? You'll never see him again!
You are my wife!

ANTONIO (SUNG)
Y caminemos por el sendero qué conce a la felicidad
Qué los dias qué no queden sean felices para ti
Caminemos caminemos mucho mas

[Constantine dances with one
of the mannequins passionately. Velázquez appears in the
doorway. Constantine dips

the mannequin, kisses it, and
puts it down. He stops, looks
at Velázquez and leaves.]

ANTONIO & MARGARET (SUNG)
Y caminemos por el sendero qué conce a la felicidad
Qué los dias qué no queden sean felices para ti
Caminemos caminemos mucho mas
Dame la mano, qué me vengo cayendo
Dame la mano, qué me vengo cayendo
Dame la mano, qué me vengo cayendo

[Cachita picks up each flow-
er and puts it in the vase.
She walks through the doorway and behind the mirror
frame.]

CACHITA
He would come home, into our room late at night. I still smell
the perfume of other women on him when he made love to
me. I still feel his hot skin and body against mine and his
beating heart pumping the blood through him. He was still
a good man, Rigo. He tried to be a good man. So I waited. I
waited for you.

[She stares straight ahead with
her flowers in her hands. Her
image slowly freezes. Rodriguez paints. She is now a reflected painting. He cries, continues to paint a portrait of her.]

END OF SCENE

ACT I - SCENE 6

RODRIGUEZ AND VELÁZQUEZ*

Rodriguez is slumped over
sitting on a rung of the ladder behind his easel. He is
dishevelled. A fresh painting
of Cachita now hangs high
on the wall above the portrait
of Constantine. Velázquez'
hat and cape hang on a hook
on the wall by the doorway.
Spanish guitar plays instru-
mental "Calderon". Billiard
balls clack.

MARGARET (V.O.)

We live as we see the sun. Our life and dreams are as one, And
living has taught me this.

[Rodriguez jumps up, disoriented. He walks through, into
the youth center to the billiard table. He sees Velázquez
playing billiards.]

Man dreams a life that is his. Until his living is done.

VELÁZQUEZ

Balls said the queen!

[Rodriguez, drunk, leans with his back against wall to keep hidden. He watches Velázquez.]

MARGARET (V.O./SUNG)

Qué toda la vida es un sueños
y los sueños son sueños tambien

[Rodriguez goes back to his apartment, searches through art supplies near the easel. He returns with a paint brush with a pointed end and holds it up like a weapon.]

RODRIGUEZ

Hold it right there!

[Rodriguez breathes heavily. Velázquez Looks up, but continues playing.]

VELÁZQUEZ

Please hold your fire... or your brush stroke.

RODRIGUEZ

You need to get the hell out of here now or I'll...

[Rodriguez staggers lunging forward and almost falls.]

VELÁZQUEZ

You're a little cranky. I probably should have asked permission before I started playing in here. Maybe we would have been off to a better start!

[He continues playing.]

RODRIGUEZ

Who are you? How did you get in here?

VELÁZQUEZ

Be reasonable, Rodriguez. I'm an old man, I don't have to answer these unimaginative questions.

RODRIGUEZ

I think you do you, you old man... shit!

[Rodriguez's voice cracks.
He loses balance and almost
falls.]

VELÁZQUEZ

You know Rodriguez, the profanity doesn't become you at all.

RODRIGUEZ

I'd hate to have to hurt you with this!

VELÁZQUEZ

Indeed! I've heard being painted to death is an horrific way to go!

RODRIGUEZ

How do you know my name? You're one of those identity thieves.

VELÁZQUEZ

Yours wouldn't be high on the list of desirable identities to steal, I'm afraid.

RODRIGUEZ

What are you doing here?

VELÁZQUEZ

It's been a long day Rodriguez. I missed my connection in Paris, then there was the ordeal with customs at JFK... shoes, cape, hat... everything had to come off. I had to throw away a brand new tube of hair gel, 32 Euros! You're lucky I made it in time to help you at all!

[Velázquez stops playing. He pulls a tobacco case and pipe out of his pocket. He sits down and begins filling the pipe with tobacco.]

RODRIGUEZ

Help me?

VELÁZQUEZ

You do seem rather desperate and sad though. So I'm going to answer one of your questions. The rest will have to wait till my jet lag subsides... or your hangover, whichever comes first.

[He lights the pipe and smokes.]

"Who are you?", you ask me. Some people spend a lifetime trying to find the answer to that question. Or for that matter, many lifetimes.

RODRIGUEZ

How about answering it in our lifetime?

VELÁZQUEZ

Time is relative, mi hijo. Two minutes, a lifetime? A little dust on the way, a frenzied extreme. Art lasts. People don't.

RODRIGUEZ

Look old man, enough riddles. I'm calling the cops!

[Velázquez smiles.]

VELÁZQUEZ

That would be unfortunate for you, Rodriguez since I believe I can be of some assistance to you.

RODRIGUEZ

Assistance? That's a joke. You're too late.

VELÁZQUEZ

Really? We don't have much confidence in our abilities, do we?

RODRIGUEZ

Copying a work isn't a question of abilities.

VELÁZQUEZ

Isn't it? Your biggest obstacle is your dead father. What a crock of shit!

RODRIGUEZ

What do you know about my father?

VELÁZQUEZ

I've done my research too.

RODRIGUEZ
The "de Silva name" is my curse.

VELÁZQUEZ
I think I may be able to help you with the replica of that "archaic royal portrait" you keep whining about.

RODRIGUEZ
No one can help me with that.

VELÁZQUEZ
Really? Not even the creator of *Las Meninas*? Take a good look Rodriguez. I Think you know who I am.

RODRIGUEZ
Look! I'm telling you...

> [Rodriguez looks at the poster *Las Meninas*. His eyes rest on Velázquez. He walks over to the hook on the wall with the hat and cape.]

VELÁZQUEZ
Hmmm?

RODRIGUEZ
I mean, how could it... Diego Velázquez?

> [Velázquez, pipe in hand, studies the poster of *Las Meninas*, laughs.]

RODRIGUEZ
No, no, no, nightmare, for sure

[Rodriguez rushes over to
look at the liquor bottle, stubs
his toe, screams in pain.]

RODRIGUEZ

Ouch, shit!

[Velázquez doesn't look at
Rodriguez.]

VELÁZQUEZ

Hmmm, relax mi hijo. Anything is possible. My good friend
Calderon says "Life is a dream and dreams themselves are
dreams!" Perhaps, in fact it is I, dreaming yoú!

RODRIGUEZ

Then I'm crazy.

VELÁZQUEZ

Yes, but I'm here anyway.

RODRIGUEZ

A 17th century painter, in my house.

VELÁZQUEZ

Indeed. If I were going to be an imposter... do you honestly
think I would choose someone who wore a get up like this?
I mean really! In south Florida heat? You'd have to be out of
your mind!

RODRIGUEZ

Velázquez!

VELÁZQUEZ

Sadly, not exactly a household name in your country, yet!

RODRIGUEZ

It depends on whose household.

VELÁZQUEZ

I could have come disguised as someone really impressive like... Spider Man for example? I bet you wouldn't have threatened to pierce him with your sharpest paint brush! Are you at least going to offer an old painter a drink?

[Rodriguez, shocked, pours
Velázquez a shot and hands it
to him. Velázquez laughs.]

By the way, I thoroughly enjoyed your little soliloquy of self-adoration earlier Rodriguez, or is it Diego?

RODRIGUEZ

I got carried away.

VELÁZQUEZ

You think you've got it all figured out already do you?

[Velázquez hands Rodriguez
a billiard cue.]

I challenge you to a game of billiards.

RODRIGUEZ

Game?

VELÁZQUEZ

Yes! While we are playing perhaps you could enlighten me on your view of how I "kissed royal ass?" Yes? It should make for some interesting conversation I suspect.

[Velázquez sips his drink.]

RODRIGUEZ

You had a king dictating your every move.

VELÁZQUEZ

Imperialism takes many forms, Rodriguez. We all have our kings we must answer to, and sometimes queens, no?

[Rodriguez laughs nervously.]

VELÁZQUEZ

What's the problem? I thought you were an excellent billiard player.

RODRIGUEZ

I'm pretty good at it.

VELÁZQUEZ

I see that you have a real billiard table. No pockets? I thought you Americans didn't call it a sport unless there were lots of little holes to put your balls into?

RODRIGUEZ

It's not so easy to find here. Besides my students, only old men play three cushion like me. I learned a long time ago, visiting my cousins in Spain.

VELÁZQUEZ

You've been to my mother country, eh?

RODRIGUEZ

Yes.

VELÁZQUEZ

Why billiards? Why not basketball, baseball, ping-pong?

RODRIGUEZ

The game is magical. It requires intellect, mathematical principles, and takes a very long time to master. It's not spectator oriented or a team sport. Without those distractions, I can focus on perfecting my skill.

VELÁZQUEZ

Indeed, learning the art of billiards, and to play well, is like learning the craft of painting. It seems a natural game for painters in fact. You learn first by imitating those you admire, quietly and methodically. You copy techniques and adopt them; some you discard. Your work begins to develop as an amalgam of artists you admire. In the process many times, you discover yourself.

> [Rodriguez takes his shot. He fumbles pushing the beads with his cue across the abacus-like string of beads to tally his score.]

RODRIGUEZ

I instruct my students on how to apply the principles, utilize their instincts, and at the same time appreciate the magic.

> [Velázquez takes the chalk, twists it over the tip of the cue stick. He takes his shot and another, then a third. He motions to Rodriguez to go.]

RODRIGUEZ

If you are who you say you are, why are you here?

[Rodriguez shoots.]

VELÁZQUEZ

If I am who I say I am, Rodriguez, wouldn't you want to know how before why?

[Rodriguez takes his second shot.]

RODRIGUEZ

How?

[Velázquez takes his shot, looks at Rodriguez with serious contemplation, balls clack twice. He takes another and a third.]

VELÁZQUEZ

You're up.

RODRIGUEZ

Oh.

[He misses.]

VELÁZQUEZ

You're overtired tonight, Rodriguez. We'll resume this game later when you're better rested.

[Velázquez takes the cue

> from Rodriguez, puts it
> down and puts his arm
> around him. They walk
> over to the diamond sys-
> tems.]

RODRIGUEZ

When I try to focus on the magical patterns, life gets in the way. Obligations, family pressures. I can't find magic in doing a replica.

> [Velázquez points with his
> pipe at Rodriguez' paint-
> ings.]

VELÁZQUEZ

Look at your paintings. You have plenty of inspiration to paint. You need to find that same inspiration for the commission.

RODRIGUEZ

The whole thing pisses me off.

VELÁZQUEZ

Picasso pissed me off.

RODRIGUEZ

What?

VELÁZQUEZ

Have you seen his 'Las Meninas'? It was said to be his tribute to my work. I saw no evidence of my influence in his horrid black and white rendition. You Americans recognize him, a newcomer, before anything I've accomplished!

I'm amazed his popularity has soared as it has. However, he did have a something to say about inspiration that be of help to you: "Inspiration exists but it has to find you while you're working."

RODRIGUEZ
Why do I need inspiration for a replica? It's a copy.

VELÁZQUEZ
Whether it be a replica, a mural or a portrait, do it with compassion, and the process in itself will be revealing.

RODRIGUEZ
Compassion?

VELÁZQUEZ
My subjects were real with struggles, pain, dreams. They had something that you don't have yet.

RODRIGUEZ
What's that?

VELÁZQUEZ
Esperenza tragica, mi hijo. Tragic hope. I remember the profound sadness of a dwarf, Maribarbóla, I painted her in *Las Meninas*. No one cared to document her story or ask her philosophy. Her gaze spoke volumes. I painted her, as well as the Infanta Margarita and the rest of the royal family. I wondered what their dreams were. They were all limited beings in some way. I found a certain beauty recognizing that sadness and hope behind it.

RODRIGUEZ
You really are Velázquez.

VELÁZQUEZ

I'm encouraged.

RODRIGUEZ

Look, I don't want to do this. I don't participate in the competition for money and power. Billiards, my students, and my girlfriend are all I have.

VELÁZQUEZ

But you have something much more important - humanity, Rodriguez. You have the compassionate humanity I've been talking about. You wouldn't be in this dilemma if you didn't. You don't want to do the replica. But you worry for your family. You don't want to disappoint them.

RODRIGUEZ

Anyone would do the same. I'm a simple man.

VELÁZQUEZ

You exemplify humanity. You encourage your girlfriend's endeavors, you mentor the young men at the youth center. You try to fulfill your family's unreasonable expectations.

RODRIGUEZ

I do what anyone would do. I treat people as I'd like to be treated.

VELÁZQUEZ

Look around! The world is teeming with vultures! What you view as ordinary consideration for fellow man is a rare quality indeed!

RODRIGUEZ

Thanks anyway, but all the humanity in the world isn't going to get this thing painted in a day!

VELÁZQUEZ

What about your girlfriend?

RODRIGUEZ

My girlfriend?

VELÁZQUEZ

Yes you remember her, 5' 4" blonde, Uruguayan decent?

RODRIGUEZ

Margaret?

VELÁZQUEZ

No Rodriguez, your other 5' 4" Uruguayan blonde girlfriend!

RODRIGUEZ

We aren't doing so great right now. She broke up with me.

VELÁZQUEZ

Your lack of personal hygiene alone could have caused that.
I've got a nice exfoliating body scrub you could try.

RODRIGUEZ

No, she's serious. There's not much I can do about it. It's not
in my hands.

VELÁZQUEZ

Really? Interesting! In whose hands is it in then?

RODRIGUEZ

You know what I mean. Her mind is made up.

VELÁZQUEZ

Sounds like your mind is made up too, hmmm? I guess you're

VELÁZQUEZ (CONT'D)
not planning to take her up on her offer then?

RODRIGUEZ
What offer?

VELÁZQUEZ
To model with her friend, to give you a couple of live bodies to ah, stimulate you into performance?

RODRIGUEZ
It's a little late for me to have "esperanza tragica" now. Her idea to model isn't going to change anything. There's no time.

VELÁZQUEZ
I think her idea is worth a go. Her music is, in fact, quite good. At times music can be the sole inspiration one needs.

RODRIGUEZ
Now you're a music connoisseur?

VELÁZQUEZ
When nobody is looking at me, like now, I reflect on the question: Wouldn't music be the only possible answer?

        [Velázquez ponders his own
        words for a moment. He
        looks over Rodriguez shoul-
        der at the blank canvas.]

Consider Margaret's support, mi hijo. Since it seems you have... nothing to lose, hmmm?

RODRIGUEZ
I have one day left to create a believable replica.

VELÁZQUEZ
Go get some sleep Rodriguez. Sleep will help you find reason.

RODRIGUEZ
So you think I'm being unreasonable?

> [Velázquez exits through doorway. Rodriguez stares at the easel. He turns to Velázquez and sees he's not there. He sits back down in a chair behind the easel. He takes another drink and begins to paint.]

MARGARET (V.O.)
Qué toda la vida es un sueño, y las sueños son sueños tambien.

END SCENE

ACT I - SCENE 7

RODRIGUEZ'S DREAM:
BAR/LITTLE HAVANA - MIAMI*

[Billiard balls clack. Velázquez wears a masquerade mask, plays billiards with Cachita and Constantine. Rodriguez stands behind easel. A self-portrait is reflected in mirror. Margaret sings. Antonio plays. The mannequins are in the bar area. Minerva sits at a table alone, smokes and drinks. She watches Margaret.]

MARGARET (SUNG)

I wanna find a secluded spot where I can meet you, hike my skirt on your lunch break and, wipe it all up with my shirt when we're done. I wanna drive around with you, for hours in the rain. Singing, stupid eighties songs at the tops of our lungs, yeah, tops of our lungs yeah.

RODRIGUEZ

When we met we talked nights, hours and years. Mostly you talked, I listened. My paintings thrived.

[Rodriguez enters, through
doorway stops and watch-
es Margaret sing. He plays
billiards with Velázquez.
His parents exit through
the doorway and stand be-
hind the frame of the mirror
and watch. Rodriguez and
Velázquez play without talking. Minerva watches Rodriguez. Margaret walks over to
Rodriguez. He lifts her onto
the table. They kiss passionately. He reaches in his pocket
and gives her a box. He pulls
a necklace out of the box and
puts it around her neck.]

RODRIGUEZ

You didn't want more then. Your voice makes everything possible. You live that way.

[He starts to make love to her
on the billiard table. Minerva
watches them. His parents
watch from behind the frame.
Velázquez continues to play
billiards around them.]

You laugh, drink, fight, intensely. You love, cry, and write intensely. Your expectations are high. I burn out. I can't keep up.

[He tries to continue making
love to her. He can't perform.

He is distracted by Minerva, Antonio, his parents,
and Velázquez. He stops and
stands up.]

RODRIGUEZ (CONT'D)
I can't sleep without your voice. I will die alone even if you're
next to me. I breathe, but too slowly. You love me a year in a
day. It's out of my hands. So I wait. I wait for you.

[Margaret sits up confused.
Rodriguez slowly walks away.
He keeps looking back. Margaret tries to stop him from
leaving. Velázquez puts down
his cue and approaches Margaret. He takes her face in
his hands and passionately
kisses her. Margaret objects
trying to keep her eyes on
Rodriguez. Rodriguez re-
turns to his easel and paints.
Velázquez makes love to her
on the table. She returns to
the stage.]

MARGARET
I wanna trace every inch of your face with my fingertips.
I wanna rest my head on your shoulders at a late morning
movie in the middle of the week, yeah, middle of the week,
yeah.

[Margaret reaches up to her
neck and grips the medal-

lion on the necklace with one hand. Minerva's gaze is downstage. Rodriguez stops painting, stands back from his easel, holds his palette. Velázquez, walks to the doorway and stops. Cachita and Constantine gaze out from the mirror.]

All characters gaze downstage mirroring the painting *Las Meninas*. Guitar ends abruptly. Sustains echoes.

END OF ACT I

ACT II - SCENE 1

BILLIARD CENTER:
MARGARET'S PLAY REHEARSAL

[Antonio plays billiards. Margaret prepares to rehearse with them. She tunes a guitar. Minerva backs in through the doorway. Her arms are loaded up with clothing. She struggles with the long trains of the dresses, dragging on the floor. Antonio comes to help her place the dresses on a table next to the billiard table. She takes out a coke for him and one for Margaret.]

MARGARET
Min, what exactly are you doing?

MINERVA
I'm trying to do what you asked.

MARGARET
What's that your carried in?

MINERVA

Costumes from the theatre!

MARGARET

For?

MINERVA

I was talking this old man at the theatre yesterday about Rodriguez's project and he told me that there had been a Spanish play there years ago called *Las Meninas*. Do you believe that, Mag?

MARGARET

The theatre had costumes? Yeah. Okay Tony, almost ready.

       [She fidgets with a guitar tuner and hand the guitar to Antonio.]

MINERVA

No! I mean isn't that ironic about the play "*Las Meninas*" and the costumes?

       [Minerva holds two fingers on each hand forming quotation marks in the air as she says "*Las Meninas*".]

MARGARET

I guess.

       [To Antonio.]

The song is in open E, wait for my cue OK?

ANTONIO

Yeah.

MINERVA

You still don't have a clue do you?

MARGARET

No. I have no idea what you're talking about, as usual.

MINERVA

Las Meninas is the painting! The replica your boyfriend is doing?

MARGARET

OK?

MINERVA

And these are costumes just like the people in the painting?

MARGARET

I've never heard of "*Las Meninas*".

> [Margaret forms quotation
> marks with her fingers sar-
> castically as she says "*Las
> Meninas*".]

Could we come back, some other time to this subject and rehearse, now, while I've got Antonio ready with his guitar?

MINERVA

You know you astound me Margaret. You should be the actor.
You act like you have no intelligence or education at all. 11th
grade Art History class, remember? King Philip IV, the princess, the dwarf, Velázquez, ring a bell? *Las Meninas*!

MARGARET

Look I didn't expect a dissertation on the painting, Min. I just thought it might motivate Rodriguez a little if we modeled. Or at least you. I thought you could stand around and rehearse your lines for the play, if nothing else. You didn't have to go this far.

MINERVA

What are you talking about? Don't you see that obviously it was meant to happen? I'm more excited now than ever! It's destiny.

MARGARET

Forget it. It's old news. Rodriguez knocked down my idea, as usual. So you won't get a chance to try out your acting, your costumes, or to realize your destiny.

MINERVA

Really? That's not what I heard.

MARGARET

What are you talking about?

MINERVA

Apparently, Rodriguez has reconsidered your idea.

MARGARET

Where did you get that?

MINERVA

Someone at the theatre told me.

MARGARET

Who?

MINERVA

I don't remember. Maybe I dreamed it. But, he was there-looking for you. Anyway, why don't you just model yourself?

MARGARET

I don't like standing still for freaking hours, okay?

MINERVA

Why me?

MARGARET

You're the actress. Besides, I thought you liked Rodriguez?

MINERVA

These are the Infanta and the dwarf costumes. Aren't they beautiful?

MARGARET

If you're into 17th century bodices I guess.

MINERVA

I know you may find this hard to believe, but your boyfriend might find you attractive in something that isn't butt tight fitting crushed velvet Lycra!

MARGARET

He's not my boyfriend, anymore. I'm trying to help him as a friend.

MINERVA

Whatever.

MARGARET

What's that supposed to mean?

MINERVA

Remember cloud nine where you've floated for the last year with your "soul mate", according to YOU? Presents every five minutes, poems, paintings, little romantic trips to the mountains? Am I supposed to believe this little moment disenchantment will stick?

MARGARET

Yes, it's going to stick. I have to keep moving forward with my plans. Rodriguez prefers to wait for his future to come to him.

[Enter Rodriguez through
Billiard Center Door. He
watches from the doorway.
No one sees him.]

MINERVA

He's worth waiting for, Mag! You're the most impatient person I know!

MARGARET

I don't want to wait. I've had a long life already. My work can't wait. It looms over me.

MINERVA

He's crazy about you. Personally, with all due respect to your creation, I'd rather have him looming over me!

MARGARET

I'm not a "diamond system." Life isn't a mathematically certain formula. I can't keep waiting for Rodriguez to get that.

MINERVA

How can you say that so easily?

MARGARET

I don't say it easily. It's something I just know. I've waited enough.

MINERVA

The man's a dream come true!

MARGARET

No Min, a dream come true is that someone comes in here in 2 1/2 minutes with a Primo-combo burrito with extra cheese and sour cream and a side of guac and chips. I'm fucking starved! Are we going to do this scene or what?

MINERVA

Try cleaning up the language, Margaret. It doesn't become you at all.

MARGARET

I'm not a tidy package, okay? I never said I was. Now can we please rehearse the carnival scene?

MINERVA

Yes Margaret, we can do the carnival scene.

MARGARET

Antonio... you come in when she says, "I think he wanted me to die." OK? Good.

> [Antonio nods. Margaret reads from the script.]

MARGARET (CONT'D)

It was...

MINERVA

It was a long time ago, back in Hungary. I'm lucky to have escaped

MARGARET

I'm lucky I escaped.

MINERVA

I know that's what it says in the script but I think what you are trying to say is better in the preterite tense. It's more sophisticated that way, so I changed it.

MARGARET

[To herself]

You've got to be kidding me!

[To Minerva]

That's thoughtful of you, really. But my character is a Hungarian immigrant. I don't think she has quite the command of the English language that you do!

MINERVA

That hurts, Mag. I assumed foolishly that you made the character Hungarian in my honor. Sadly, you forget that my paternal grandparents were Hungarian immigrants! I don't think that you hear me talk in an overly simplistic way, do you?

MARGARET

Will you just read from the freaking script?

MINERVA (Sarcastically to herself.)
Suit yourself.

> [Minerva rolls her eyes.
> Rodriguez laughs. Antonio
> fidgets, bored, and looks at
> his watch.]

It all started after Mama died. My papa was drinking more
and more. We had an act in a the traveling circus. But after
Mama was gone, the act was finished.

> [Rodriguez continues to watch
> unnoticed. Margaret reads
> stage directions from script.]

MARGARET
She holds back tears at the mention of her mother. She shakes
her head. Okay Min go!

MINERVA
So papa decided to make this spectacle. He would tie me to a
spinning wheel, give it a hard pull, step back, tie a blindfold
over his eyes and throw knives at me. Every time he would
drink more and more before the show. I would think. "I'm
going to die this time"...

> [Margaret holds one finger
> up to Antonio.]

MINERVA
I think he wanted me to die.

MARGARET
Excellent. Go Tony!

[Minerva sees Rodriguez. She
looks down embarrassed. He's
watching Margaret. Antonio
plays intro to "Cockpit".]

MARGARET (SUNG)

*You got what you wanted. But you can't have what you got. So
go ahead, flaunt it, I won't be what you're not*

[Margaret notices Antonio
is distracted and looking at
the door behind her. She sees
Rodriguez and motions to
him to stop playing.]

MARGARET

Let's take a five minute cigarette break okay? Good job.

[To Rodriguez.]

Hi.

RODRIGUEZ

Hi.

MARGARET

We'll be out your way in a few minutes.

RODRIGUEZ

You're not in my way bab... I mean, I'm not working with the
guys today.

MARGARET

What are you doing?

RODRIGUEZ

Trying to paint. I enjoyed watching the rehearsal. It's coming finally, huh? It's going to be great, Mag.

MARGARET

Thanks... I gotta go back to rehearsal.

RODRIGUEZ

Wait. I've been thinking about what you said.

MARGARET

About what?

RODRIGUEZ

Letting you model and maybe that will help me get this replica together.

MARGARET

It wasn't "letting" me, Rigo. I've got plenty of stuff to do. It's not like you're doing me any favors.

RODRIGUEZ

Obviously, baby, come on. I know you care about it. The foundation is coming to check on my progress. I'm running out of time.

MARGARET

When did you figure that out? We're all running out of time.

RODRIGUEZ

I don't like to concentrate on that so much.

MARGARET

So why the sudden decision?

RODRIGUEZ
Why so suspicious, analyzing? Does it matter why?

MARGARET
Yeah, it does. I put a lot of energy into getting your ideas flowing. So I'd like to know who or what made you see what I've said all along.

RODRIGUEZ
I decided to do it. Nothing more. You're searching again for things that aren't there.

MARGARET
I heard that you were at the theatre looking for me

RODRIGUEZ
I went there to see if we could talk.

MARGARET
What about?

RODRIGUEZ
How weird it feels not to have you around. I missed you last night.

MARGARET
You're right. I'm searching for something that isn't there. If you can't have the drive to seize something as important as this, then we have nothing in common.

RODRIGUEZ
Let's not do this baby... it's not good for us, you're making everything so hard.

RODRIGUEZ

What's all this?

[He points to the costumes.]

MINERVA

Costumes from the theatre. I heard there was once a play there called *Las Meninas*! I thought that, since you've decided to accept Mag's offer for us to model, I'd use them! Aren't they magnificent!

RODRIGUEZ

What do you mean since I "decided to?"

MINERVA

Well, I heard you were at the theatre and that you changed your mind about...

RODRIGUEZ

I was at the theatre. But not for that reason, for something else.

> [He looks at Margaret. She talks to the guys and looks at the script. He takes one of the billiard balls in his hand moving it in a triangular shape. He studies the balls.]

RODRIGUEZ

What do you know about the play?

MINERVA

It's called *Las Meninas*, a fictional work by Antonio Buero Vallejo. I've researched him too. He's a Spanish playwright
from the Franco era who was imprisoned during the Spanish
Civil War and sentenced to death but fortunately he...

> [Rodriguez stops moving the
> ball abruptly. He keeps his
> eyes down on the table.]

RODRIGUEZ

Thanks for your ideas. I'll take these over to my apartment

> [He takes the costumes in
> his arms. He walks toward
> the door.]

MINERVA

Rodriguez are you all right?

RODRIGUEZ

Yeah, I'm fine. I gotta get back to work.

> [He backs around, pushes the
> door open, and exits. Miner-
> va calls to him.]

MINERVA

When do you need me to model?

RODRIGUEZ (V.O.)

Later.

MINERVA

OK!

[To herself.]

Oh my God, Margaret's crazy. He's a dream.

MARGARET

Ready to do the carnival scene all the way through?

[Margaret looks around.]

Where's Rigo?

MINERVA

He left pretty abruptly.

[To herself.]

Strange.

MARGARET

He's gotten himself in a corner now. The clock's ticking.

MINERVA

Did you kiss and make up? He seems so sad without you.

[To herself.]

Why, I'm sure I don't know.

MARGARET

It's over, I told you.

[Antonio shoots.]

MINERVA

You're crazy and I guarantee you're going to regret it if you let him get away.

MARGARET

Did you two work out a time for you to model?

MINERVA

Sort of. Mag are you not listening? You're making a big mistake. I know what you're doing and it's wrong, making him pay for other guys' mess ups.

MARGARET

Look, Rigo needs to learn that apathy has consequences.

MINERVA

Maybe you need to learn to let people do things on their own terms and in their own time.

MARGARET

Thanks for the unsolicited analysis. Tomorrow's rehearsal will include my analysis of your love life.

MINERVA

That should be pretty brief.

MARGARET

OK, let's take the carnival scene from where we left off. Ready?

[Minerva prematurely launches into delivering her lines.]

MINERVA

So papa decided to make this spectacle. He would tie me to a spinning wheel, give it a hard pull, step back, tie a blindfold over his eyes and throw knives at me. Every time he would drink more and more before the show. I would think. "I'm going to die this time". I think he wanted me to die.

[Antonio plays billiards.]

MARGARET

Tony, come on, that's your cue!

Billiard balls crack.

END OF SCENE

ACT II - SCENE 2

RODRIGUEZ'S STUDIO*

Lights come up on Rodriguez's studio through the doorway.

[Rodriguez is in his apartment. He puts the costumes on the mannequins that stand near the easel. He pours a shot of rum; he stands, and contemplates the costumes. He walks to his easel and paints a couple of final strokes on a painting of Margaret. He stares at the easel. Margaret appears in the Mirror.]

MARGARET
My parents fled Uruguay. Military stormed their little business and took everything. So they came here, with nothing. Are you listening Rigo?

RODRIGUEZ
I know this story, Mag. You've told me before.

MARGARET

They believed this was a place of limitless opportunities. They worked hard. I was born. They encouraged me to believe in myself, to be spontaneous and think on my feet.

RODRIGUEZ

Everyone isn't so fortunate. My father believed I should be as little like me as possible. What does this have to do with anything?

MARGARET

I fell flat on my face so many times. Every time they'd tell me to pick myself up and try again. They gave me hope. Dreaming was a luxury they didn't have.

RODRIGUEZ

I can't be someone I'm not. Not for you, or for Papa. It's not possible. But I can wait. I am patient. I will wait for you.

MARGARET

You are beautiful to me, methodical and certain. Life is urgent, a dream is important. I love you Rigo. But, I can't wait for you. I may never grow old.

> [Rodriguez finishes the painting. He takes it off the easel and puts it on the floor next to the *Las Meninas* poster. He puts blank canvas on his easel, sits on a rung of the ladder. Enter Velázquez. He stands in the doorway smoking his pipe.]

VELÁZQUEZ

A night's sleep did some good, espero?

[Rodriguez stares straight
ahead at his canvas.]

RODRIGUEZ

She's not coming back.

VELÁZQUEZ

Your profound feeling for humanity, it's getting in the way,
distracting you from your work.

RODRIGUEZ

You said my humanity is my strength as an artist! Now you
say it's a weakness.

VELÁZQUEZ

An obstacle can be your greatest inspiration.

RODRIGUEZ

How am I supposed overcome my "humanity"?

VELÁZQUEZ

Die!

[Rodriguez bristles.]

It certainly freed me up for the afternoon. Didn't it?

[Rodriguez laughs, relieved.]

RODRIGUEZ

Did she ever paint?

VELÁZQUEZ

Who?

RODRIGUEZ

The Infanta. Did you teach her how to paint?

VELÁZQUEZ

No.

RODRIGUEZ

Did she grow old?

VELÁZQUEZ

No, she didn't.

RODRIGUEZ

What happened to her?

[Velázquez stops smoking.]

VELÁZQUEZ

She died, in childbirth with her seventh child. She was twenty.

[Rodriguez drops his head.
Velázquez puts his arm
around him. They cross
through the wall between
Rodriguez's apartment and
the Billiard Center to the billiard table.]

RODRIGUEZ

You were her father's favorite painter, and mine.

[Rodriguez takes a cue and
shoots.]

VELÁZQUEZ
I would be disappointed if you despised my work due to
your father's admiration of it. Yet, I would be as disappointed if you liked it for the same reason.

RODRIGUEZ
My father doesn't really know who I am.

VELÁZQUEZ
Perhaps you don't really know who he is.

RODRIGUEZ
I'm sure he doesn't want me to know. He wants to remind
me that I'm not measuring up to his expectations.

VELÁZQUEZ
I suspect that his pressure is forcing you to find capabilities
you never imagined you had.

RODRIGUEZ
So far I'm a disaster. Tomorrow the foundation will come
and see an empty canvas.

VELÁZQUEZ
Mira, hijo mio, it is sometimes quite difficult to discern between inspiration and imitation...

[Velázquez points to the *Las
Meninas* poster.]

...humanity and apathy...

RODRIGUEZ

I hate him.

> [Velázquez points to the por-
> trait of Constantine with his
> pipe.]

VELÁZQUEZ

...between love and hate...

> [He points to the doorway.]

...reality and dreams, 300 years, or a day. They are all connected, truths that have always been here. Just as we artists are
connected, the same geometrical patterns in our works and in
your diamond systems can be found in all of life's mysteries.

> [Rodriguez shoots and turns
> to Velázquez. He is gone. He
> looks at the empty doorway.
> He walks to the easel. He sits
> behind it, smoking. Billiard
> balls crack.]

END SCENE

ACT II - SCENE 3

MINERVA AND RODRIGUEZ

[Rodriguez sits and paints behind easel. There's a knock on the apartment door. Rodriguez does not respond. There is a second knock. Rodriguez does not answer. Minerva enters.]

MINERVA

I'm here to model now Rodriguez.

RODRIGUEZ

I know.

MINERVA

Have you made progress?

[She puts her bag and script down on the table.]

RODRIGUEZ

Yeah, four paintings in twenty-four hours. I'm painting everything but what I'm supposed to paint.

MINERVA

Everything? Really? Or an endless series of portraits of "Princess" Margaret?

> [Rodriguez continues to stare at the canvas. Minerva unbuttons the costume from the mannequin and pulls it off from the top.]

May I use your bathroom?

> [She begins to unbutton the back of her shirt.]

RODRIGUEZ

I don't know how safe it is at the moment.

MINERVA

Your bathroom's dangerous?

> [She laughs and exits with costume in hand.]

RODRIGUEZ

You know, clean.

MINERVA (V.O.)

Margaret said you're stuck.

RODRIGUEZ

True.

MINERVA (V.O.)

She wants you to succeed, you know.

RODRIGUEZ

I don't think it matters now.

MINERVA

You mean since you're stuck?

RODRIGUEZ

Yeah, since I'm stuck. No matter what I do it's going to piss somebody off. I have no real choices.

MINERVA (V.O.)

If you choose to think that!

RODRIGUEZ

I didn't choose the circumstances, my parents' foundation or Margaret's expectations.

[He picks up his palette and continues painting.]

MINERVA (V.O.)

You can whine and intellectualize, or you can make something out of the situation.

[Minerva returns in costume. Rodriguez looks up stunned.]

Mother used to say, "If you can't find the choice that will make you happy, choose the one that's the least painful."

RODRIGUEZ
Actually that makes sense.

MINERVA
Life involves suffering Rodriguez. It's unavoidable.

RODRIGUEZ
There's nothing I can do about it.

MINERVA
You view many things as out of your control. You don't even attempt things that are well within your reach. Margaret, assumes that all is possible. When she's told she has no chance of succeeding it only further fuels her determination. She dreams and relentlessly pursues.

RODRIGUEZ
She's not coming back.

[Rodriguez hangs the portrait
of Margaret on the wall.]

MINERVA
If you accept it that easily, then perhaps your assumptions are correct.

RODRIGUEZ
She has pulled away from me, far away.

MINERVA
So you give up hope. I get up everyday hoping that if I wash my face and smile, maybe I'll be seen, noticed, acknowledged.

[She turns to the mirror and
fixes her hair. Rodriguez approaches her]

RODRIGUEZ

You are talented, Minerva.

MINERVA

And loved? Adored? No. I'm like your students in the youth
center. They are invisible, cute, irrelevant. I see hope in their
eyes though. Not happiness, but tragic hope.

RODRIGUEZ

[To himself.]

Esperanza tragica!

[He stares at her mesmerized.]

MINERVA

I see the same look in the eyes of those in *Las Meninas*. There
are inescapable realities in their eyes, rich or poor, homely or
lovely.

RODRIGUEZ

You are lovely.

MINERVA

It seems to be the premise of Velázquez's work, from what I
can tell. It's a necessity of survival, of existence. Hope.

RODRIGUEZ

Amidst adversity

MINERVA

Amidst life. Hope is found in a painting or a song.

> [Minerva tears a little cor-
> ner of a pizza box. She writes
> something on it. She kisses
> it and puts it in down the
> front of her dress. Rodriguez
> paints.]

RODRIGUEZ

What are you writing on all those little pieces of paper?

MINERVA

Quotes. I like to write things down. I look at them at the end of
the day and paste them into my journal. Here's one you can keep.

> [She pulls the cardboard shred
> out of the front of her dress
> and puts it down on the little
> table. Rodriguez paints. Min-
> erva walks to the *Las Meninas*
> poster. She studies it.]

> Velázquez gave light to people
> usually considered unimpor-
> tant, misfits who are over-
> looked or underestimated.
> I'm one of them, a misfit in
> the shadows.

RODRIGUEZ

People worth knowing are there. They aren't caught up in the
rat race. I can't find my way out. I'm fucked up. I can't see
right now.

MINERVA

You'd be surprised at the things that go on right in front of me and those of us who are not attractive, or are damaged in some way. We don't count. But with that unimportance comes clarity.

RODRIGUEZ

Everything has become blurred. I can't listen to her voice now. It used to have answers.

MINERVA

The answers are there in front of you. The blind have keen vision. Those of us left alone in the darkness see the light more clearly.

RODRIGUEZ

Then I belong there too.

[Rodriguez walks over to her
and stands very close.]

I always try to stay in the shadows as much as possible.

MINERVA

For you it's a choice, not a condition. You can go back into the light whenever you please. That's the difference between you and me.

[Minerva moves away.]

RODRIGUEZ

My darkest moments have been in broad daylight. Some of my loneliest have been in the most crowded places.

[He moves toward her again

and strokes her face. He takes her face in his hands and passionately kisses her. Rushed, he pushes her backwards against the billiard table and unbuttons the back of her dress. Minerva starts to embrace him. Her opens hands clench to fists. She pounds his back and violently pushes him away.]

MINERVA

What are you doing? You're right. You are fucked up. Am I that pathetic to you?

RODRIGUEZ

No, Minerva! I didn't mean to!

MINERVA

How convenient to have a sad and hopeful starry eyed admirer here to help you get over Margaret! I'm so stupid.

[Her voice begins to crack.]

RODRIGUEZ

No, it isn't that! Please wait! Listen!

MINERVA

It's tempting. I could pretend for some moments. Pretend that you see something in me.

RODRIGUEZ

I do Minerva. I would never hurt you.

[Minerva cries.]

MINERVA

I could close my eyes and make love to you. But when I opened them yours would be closed too.

RODRIGUEZ

I was out of line. It was wrong.

MINERVA

My feelings have been written all over my face, haven't they? So you took advantage of me, because you could. I'm an easy mark.

RODRIGUEZ

I'm so sorry.

MINERVA

What's the matter? I'm not responding the way you expected? I came here because I saw a good man with talent. Someone who needs inspiration, encouragement. You confuse hopefulness with weakness. I do have some fucking dignity. I have that!

> [She grabs her purse. She
> runs out through the door-
> way, wearing the costume,
> crying.]

RODRIGUEZ

Let me explain. Minerva!

> [He runs and tries to stop
> her. He notices her clothes

left on the table and takes
them.]

RODRIGUEZ (CONT'D)
You left your clothes.

[He turns around and throws
the clothes down.]

That's great you idiot! You ass-hole! Ass-hole!

[He kicks the *Las Meninas*
poster across the floor. Pulls
the portraits of his father and
Margaret off the wall and
throws then down. He kicks
the pile of clothes on the
floor. Minerva's cardboard
quote flies up out of them. He
stops, picks it up and reads
it.]

When nobody is looking at me, like now, I reflect on the question: Wouldn't music be the only possible answer?

[He breaks down, crying, his
head in his hands. He begins
to paint.]

END OF SCENE

ACT II - SCENE 4

MINERVA'S WHEEL*

[Rodriguez paints. The painting is projected from behind the scrim of the mirror. It's portrait of Minverva, wearing angel wings, and holding a mirror. Margaret is in the painting also. She's lying nude on her side, facing the mirror. Rodriguez hangs the painting on the wall. Billiard balls crack. Enter Velázquez, wears a masquerade mask. He pushes a platform with an upright big wheel painted with many colors. The wheel pictured in the Hermetist painting from King Philip's palace. Minerva enters. She wears the Maribárbola costume. She methodically pushes the step ladder to the wheel and mounts it. She stands in a jumping jack po-

> sition on two pegs. Her hands
> grip the other two pegs over
> her head. Antonio plays.
> Velázquez bows to King Phil-
> ip and Queen Mariana re-
> flected in the mirror. He nods
> to audience.]

MARGARET (V.O./SUNG)

You got what you wanted. But you can't have what you got.
So go ahead, flaunt it. I won't be what you're not.
Wheel keeps spinning, round and round.
It takes her upside down.
Daddy's beaming, he's so proud.
Makes you wanna wring her neck.
You know you gotta wring her neck.

> [Velázquez walks up to the
> wheel and gives it a full tug
> causing her to rock from
> side to side. The wheel slows.
> Minerva, addresses Rodri-
> guez.]

MINERVA

You had it all, both of you. Nobody noticed, I was there. It's okay, I don't resent you for it. We'll all die someday. We're equal on that day. All that we'll leave behind are our creations, little remnants of lives lived: *Las Meninas*, your mother's child, your painting, songs and tiny words on shreds of paper.

> [Velázquez approaches the
> wheel and pulls it harder this

time. It slowly spins Minerva around. He steps back
far from the spinning wheel
and throws knives at her as
she spins. He bows with each
successive throw of the knife.
The king and queen applaud.]

MARGARET (V.O./SUNG)
Ardent bravado, you should take your pill
So crawl across the floor to her
Your destiny's fulfilled
Wheel keeps spinning round and round
It takes her upside down
Daddy's beaming, he's so proud
Makes you wanna wring her neck,
you know you gotta wring her neck.

MINERVA
From my darkness you were illuminated. I knew your bril-
liance Rigo. So did she. She was vibrant, but in a hurry. So
neither of you really saw. You could have seen it if you were
invisible like me. She waits for no one and expects everything.
I expect nothing, but hope for the improbable, and I wait for
you.

[Velázquez walks back to his
place and takes a long swig
from a bottle. He calls Rodriguez to come. He blind-
folds Rodriguez. Rodriguez
throws the last knife. It goes
through Minerva's heart. Her
body goes limp.]

MARGARET (V.O./SUNG)
I got what I wanted. But I can't have what I got.
The task made you feel daunted.
So you had to pull it out.

[Music abruptly stops. The king and queen applaud heartily. Velázquez bows for them. The wheel stops. The king and queen exit, then Velázquez. Margaret, enters. She's wearing the Infanta costume. She pulls the knife out of Minerva's heart. Minerva's body slumps over onto Margaret. Rodriguez removes his blindfold and sees Minerva's limp body and tries to help. Antonio and Margaret push wheel with Minerva off stage.]

END OF SCENE

ACT II - SCENE 5

RODRIGUEZ'S FINAL DREAM:
MADRID, 1660/MIAMI 1997

Billiard balls clack.

CACHITA (V.O.)
Rigo, the foundation directors are at the door. They've come to see your progress.

[Rodriguez is alone in his studio. The Infanta from Rodriguez's replica of *Las Meninas* is reflected in the mirror. Some other details from the replica are also finished. He talks to the canvas.]

RODRIGUEZ
Mag, I try to cry out for you. No sound will come. I hear your voice, so clearly, that I can't even hear my own. I move slowly, so you leave me behind. But I am moving. I am finding my way. I never told you I love you. You were always in a hurry. I do. I'll be here; I'll be okay.

[Enter Margaret in the Infanta costume. She kisses Rodriguez passionately. She walks to the billiard table and with her back to Rodriguez, she takes off the Infanta costume. She wears a backless black dress. She climbs onto the billiard table and lies on her side facing the diamond systems poster.]

[Enter Velázquez. He stands in the doorway calls to Rodriguez, he addresses him as Juan. He's weak.]

VELÁZQUEZ

Finally inspired?

RODRIGUEZ

Come, look. Thanks to you I've been able to work. Let me get this out of the way.

[Rodriguez moves the ladder out of the way.]

VELÁZQUEZ

No, hijo mio. It won't be necessary. I won't be painting now. It was, in fact, quite an arduous journey from France.

RODRIGUEZ

I know you're not going to paint, but, I wanted to show you my progress... on the replica...

[He studies Velázquez.]

VELÁZQUEZ
Any news from the inquiry commission?

[Velázquez coughs. He takes
out his pipe and tobacco,
packs it and lights it.]

RODRIGUEZ
You mean the foundation?

VELÁZQUEZ
Get me a wine.

[Velázquez walks to the
billiard table. Rodriguez
goes to him and gives him
a drink. Rodriguez takes
down two cues. Velázquez
declines.]

VELÁZQUEZ
No, you play now, without me, Juan.

RODRIGUEZ
Juan?

[Rodriguez reluctantly plays
alone around Margaret.]

VELÁZQUEZ
The truce between France and Spain is now in force since the
wedding. King Philip can now turn his attention to procuring

VELÁZQUEZ (CONT'D)
my acceptance for the Order of Santiago.

[Velázquez coughs more
now. Rodriguez gets up to
help him.]

I shall wear it proudly to the next royal marriage of the Duke
of Austria and the Infanta Margarita... your muse in the
paintings? Isn't she?

RODRIGUEZ
Why did you help me?

[King Philip appears in the
frame of the mirror.]

KING PHILIP
Diego! You've returned. We received the confirmation from
the inquiry into your bloodline. Your bloodline is pure. You
are officially accepted into the Royal Order of Santiago. Con-
gratulations.

[The king turns around
from behind the frame of
the mirror and exits. *Las
Meninas* is reflected in the
mirror. Velázquez coughs
more, collapses. Reina Mariana comes to help him. She
becomes Cachita.]

VELÁZQUEZ
Rodriguez!

[Rodriguez runs to the mirror and paints the red Cross of Santiago on Velázquez's reflection.]

VELÁZQUEZ (CONT'D)

Thank you, my son.

[Velázquez's head drops back down. King Philip becomes Constantine. He enters through the doorway. He carries a little child's easel and puts it down on the floor in front of the billiard table. He walks over to Rodriguez in front of the easel.]

CÓNSTANTINE

Rodriguez, you've completed the replica, as well you should.

RODRIGUEZ

Papa?

CONSTANTINE

Your father was a magnificent painter. I had never seen such talent. Your mother was like a school girl. I could see the enchantment in her eyes when we would see him painting out in the streets of Havana. He illuminated her. I wanted her to look at me with those same eyes. I loved her. What could I offer her? How could I win? I didn't have his talent or charm.

RODRIGUEZ

What are you saying Papa?

CONSTANTINE

But he couldn't be a real father to you. He couldn't offer you a life in the United States of America! No! That costs money. I had that. I was sure you both would grow to love me. You didn't. If it weren't for you, your mother would have denied herself all I offered. But for you, she denied herself love; The man of her dreams.

RODRIGUEZ

No Papa! Mama? Mama, why? Your whole life? A lifetime Mama, my lifetime!

CONSTANTINE

You are so much like him, your father. Your paintings are so much like his, they bring me nothing but pain. I gave you both a name, the deSilva name! At least I deserve some respect don't I? I deserve it from you! I demand it. So I waited. I waited for you.

[Rodriguez tries to cry out but his voice is strained.]

RODRIGUEZ

Mama!

[Cachita gets up slowly. She stands next to Constantine in front of the mirror.]

There's a knock on the door.

CACHITA

Rigo, the foundation directors are at the door. They've come to see your progress. I'm proud of you mi hijo.

[Enter Antonio with clip board. He walks to the large easel with Rodriguez's replica and silently write notes.]

RODRIGUEZ

We do what we have to do to get through. But just like you, I have to fall. Papa is still my papa even though he isn't.

[Minerva wearing angel wings and the Maribárbola costume walks slowly to Rodriguez's painting of Venus on the wall and takes it down. The Cross of Santiago Rodriguez painted on it remains. She holds it resting on the billiard table. Rodriguez touches her face gently.]

I can see my reflection clearly But in the end, just like you, I had to find my own way.

[Rodriguez to Velázquez]

Just like you, my blood is pure. And just like you, I'm still who I've known I was all along.

[Velázquez stands slowly. Rodriguez happily returns to his easel to paint. Antonio puts down his clip board, walks over to his guitar and begins to play. The manne-

quins and chunks of rock
float. They remain suspend-
ed over the billiard table with
Margaret on it. Rodriguez
continues to paint oblivious
to the others. Margaret jumps
off of the billiard table with
her script in hand.]

MARGARET

Scene. That was good guys. Let's take it all the way through
one more time.

All characters freeze except
Rodriguez. Guitar music resumes of "La Vida es Sueño."
Slowly Cachita exits through
Court Door, Constantine exits next, Antonio and Minerva next. Then Margaret exits
happily through the Court
Door. Velázquez does not
remove his gaze from Rodriguez who continues to paint.
He slowly walks to the Court
Door, pauses to look at Rodriguez, then exits. Rodriguez
turns to the Court Door just
after Velázquez exits. He removes his painting from the
easel. He grabs his bag and
the painting under his arm
and pauses at his apartment
door for a moment. He turns

out the lights and exits. Music stops.

THE END

Jacinta Chaminade is a proud member of The Dramatists Guild of America.

About the Author

Jennifer's body of artistic works includes: dramas, musicals, comedies, a one-woman show, and five original albums that uncover characters with an invincible human heart. Her performances, collaboration and studies have taken her to France, Spain, Senegal, and most recently, Oaxaca, Mexico.

She has a B.A. in International Studies and French from the University of North Florida and an M.F.A. in Creative Writing from the University of New Orleans.
She is a professor of Humanities, English, and Creative Writing at Florida State College at Jacksonville.
She is inspired by her family, her travels and by people with whom she spontaneously shares a meal, a story, or a song along the way.

Other works by the Author

Artichoke Soup

Eva Chase Wood?

Handmaid

Renunciant

Pietà

Cracking la Coque

Majigeen - a musical

La Caroline - a rock opera

Original Music

kid jail

Famadihana

Marjorie's Wake

Artichoke Soup

Majigeen (single)

Also streaming on Spotify, Amazon Music,
Apple Music
For more information, visit
www.jacintachaminade.com
www.ajennda.org
www.jennchase.com

www.ingramcontent.com/pod-product-compliance
Lightning Source LLC
Chambersburg PA
CBHW051345020726
47501CB00007B/2271